THE SNIPER

A.S. MOST

Publisher's Cataloging-In-Publication Data
(Prepared by The Donohue Group, Inc.)
Names: Most, A. S., author.
Title: The sniper / A.S. Most.
Description: First Stillwater River Publications edition. | Paw-
    tucket, RI, USA : Stillwater River Publications, [2020]
Identifiers: ISBN 9781952521638 (paperback)
Subjects: LCSH: Criminal snipers--New York (State)--Fiction.
    | Neo-Nazis--New York (State)--Fiction. | Reporters and
    reporting--New York (State)--Fiction. | Murder--Investi-
    gation--New York (State)--Fiction. | LCGFT: Detective
    and mystery fiction. | Thrillers (Fiction)
Classification: LCC PS3613.O7885 S65 2020 | DDC 813/.6--
    dc23

Also by A.S. Most

No Loose Ends

A Deadly Cover

PROLOGUE

Where to draw the line? People may despise others, but going so far as to take that person's life is where most people in America draw the line. Our humanity keeps us in check.

We suspend that inhibition when we declare war. The line is wiped away. Killing is how that 'game' is played. Anyone remotely supportive of the enemy is disposable. The Israelis have declared there is no safe harbor for Hezbollah, their sworn Palestinian enemy. If they fire rockets into Israel from a residential building, the Israelis consider the building a fair target, regardless of its regular occupants. They don't make an effort to sort out the building's occupants and only inflict their fire on actual rocket firing personnel. War is war.

The neo-Nazis from time to time attack and kill Jews indiscriminately. The Jews do not launch a like response. The 'war' is fought on an uneven field. One side does the killing; the other mourns its losses. The 'line' not crossed by the Jews eliminates one possible deterrent to the killing.

For one man that line was about to be crossed.

CHAPTER ONE

Another terrorist attack. This time in Albany, New York. The synagogue was tightly guarded, but the killers were well-armed and knew how to neutralize the guards. Once they were past the protected entryway the congregation inside was easy prey. It would be like shooting fish in a barrel.

The two shooters quietly climbed to separate sides of the balcony overlooking the small congregation below. The balcony was empty, as their reconnaissance the week before had indicated it would be. Time was precious because the two guards' bodies would soon be discovered.

The shooters nodded their heads in agreement and opened fire on the people below. The AK-47s unleashed a withering fire on the human targets. People screamed and fell but no one escaped. Running for the large entry to exit was futile. The shooters were especially careful about preventing any congregants from escaping and focused their shooting on people seeking to escape through the entrance.

In two minutes all eighteen people were dead or dying. The shooters quickly ran downstairs, tossing papers with swastikas into the air, and walked calmly out to their car. A few passing pedestrians paid them no mind.

The evening news was taken over by the bloody event. The police had no leads but it was unmistakably a terrorist act. Cries of outrage were coming from all the usual quarters. The president was shocked by the carnage, along with the rest of the nation.

Several passersby now recalled seeing two men leaving the synagogue around the time of the shooting. Each described Caucasian males dressed casually and seemingly in no hurry to get into their waiting car. The few witnesses took no notice of anything the men might have been carrying.

Bert Alder and his wife, Terry, watched the terrible aftermath on TV. They sat in stony silence.

CHAPTER TWO

The early autumn evening was pleasantly cool in the Bronx. Gus Oren was wrapping up his last brake job. The paperwork was a pain, but wasn't difficult for a simple brake lining replacement. He was looking forward to meeting his friends at Norton's Pub and raising a brew to toast the guys who carried out the synagogue shooting one week ago. He cleaned up his work area in the service center and changed into jeans and a sweatshirt with torn-off sleeves. He was proud of the tattoos that adorned his arms so he wore no jacket. As leader of the local Americans for America group, he was quick to come forward and defend any action against what he perceived as foreign elements in the society. Jews ranked near the top of his list of non-Americans who were hurting his country.

He was the last man out, so he locked the door. The showroom was next door and would be open for another two hours. His car was parked just inside the small parking area near the service entrance. He whistled a tune as he approached the car. That last event in his life passed very quickly.

Two shots were fired from a deserted lot across the street. Either one would have sufficed. They both entered the center of his chest and were immediately fatal. A salesman in the showroom heard the shots and went outside to see if there was any damage to the cars in the large used car lot. He discovered the body and called the police.

There were no clues to explain why Oren was killed. The police had nothing to go on. His well-known neo-Nazi views and the timing of his murder, one week after the recent killings in Albany, were considered remote tie-ins. The synagogue killings had taken place two hundred miles away.

CHAPTER THREE

Police calls were sometimes the lead to a story and Leslie Nugent had hit a brief dry spell. She was hungry for a lead. Her year at *The Times* had been very productive. Her story about a toxic drug and the many killings related to the cover-up of its manufacture had been a coup. She was now a highly regarded investigative reporter. Nevertheless, here she was, sitting in her apartment, eating a hastily assembled dinner of leftover Chinese food, listening in on police calls looking for a lead like some junior reporter new to the staff.

The murder of a neo-Nazi leader was interesting but it offered no leads to follow. Coming close on the heels of the synagogue shooting it raised the possibility of a revenge murder, but the victim in this case had no obvious connection with the synagogue killings. She tucked this one away for future reference.

Leslie's one-bedroom apartment in an old four story walk-up brownstone was in a slowly gentrifying area of upper Manhattan. The apartment needed a lot of updating but her lease didn't include any updates. She accepted the apartment's age and was satisfied that the building was reasonably well cared for. Sure, there was a lot of paint peeling off the ceiling and the bathtub and sink in the bathroom had big rust stains. A number of tiles in the bathroom floor were missing. The place was old. The building was waiting its turn to be sold and then modernized. She hoped she'd be able to afford the next lease.

Tonight she sat on her bed pondering her most recent romantic failure. On reflection, she seemed to start off okay with good guys, but didn't seem to have the emotional stamina to go over the goal line. She hated the sports analogies, but in her case they seemed apt. Her inability to combine a strong work commitment with serious romance was disturbing. She wasn't giving up, but hoped the next time she was rounding third (*another sports cliché*, she thought) she'd find a way to let her guy know he was number one and her career, second, even if a very close second.

Tonight she was dwelling on this issue in her life. That wasn't the case every night. She had friends, male and female, with whom she frequently socialized so she wasn't living a depressed, house-bound lifestyle. Her ego was stroked often enough to reassure her that she shouldn't be overly concerned. She was attractive, bright, held down a highly desirable job at one of the world's top newspapers and had been romanced by some very desirable guys. Still, here she was, alone and wondering why. Self-doubt was bound to slip in every once in a while. As long as it didn't hang around too long she could shake it off.

CHAPTER FOUR

Several weeks later, in the South Bronx, Merrill Davis, a line repairman for the electric company that serviced that section of the city, was sent out to repair a downed power line that was reported over the phone. He couldn't find the downed line where he was told it would be. False alarm calls were uncommon but not unheard of. Sitting in his truck and writing up the nuisance call, a single rifle shot from a tenement across the street smashed through his driver's side window, entered his left temple, and exited the right side of his skull. The bullet then lodged in the padded portion of the passenger side door.

The police responded quickly but could do nothing for the dead driver. Forensic police determined where the shot came from, given the path the bullet traveled through the truck and driver. They searched the partly occupied building and deduced which apartment the shot was fired from. The apartment, they learned, had long been deserted. Nothing

7

turned up to identify a suspect and no witnesses could offer useful information.

Lieutenant Lionel Cobb, the lead homicide detective on the case, could see that this was destined to be another unsolved murder in a very rough neighborhood. Two things did stand out, however. First, the downed line was non-existent, suggesting the repairman was lured there to be killed, and second, Davis was an outspoken neo-Nazi, a leader who organized street protests against minority groups. That was all he had. No leads but possibly a hate crime. A hate crime in reverse.

CHAPTER FIVE

The waiting room of his group's medical office was jammed as usual at 2:00 p.m. With six busy internists and pediatricians sharing the space it was just barely adequate. Bert had learned that any complaint would be met by the practice manager with some variation on the theme that this was all the space they could afford.

He mused how the surgeons upstairs left their waiting space empty much of the day, but while it was empty they were busy pulling diamonds out of the earth in the OR. They could afford whatever they wanted, working on patients that Bert and his colleagues found for them. The wealth gap troubling the country extended even into the medical profession. As a pediatrician he had accepted the fact that he would be among the low earners in the group.

By five thirty he and two of his partner pediatricians, Monica Lorenz and Ellis Collins, were hanging up their white coats in their small offices. He looked in on Monica's office.

9

"Any interest in a beer on the way home? I need to decompress."

The much younger Monica gave him a smile and, surprisingly, agreed to his suggestion, "Meet you at the bar in Louis' Char House. Didja ask Ellis?"

"Yes, indeed, and to no one's surprise the young father is heading home to help his wife put together dinner."

"See you there in fifteen minutes, Bert."

Bert had long considered making a move on Monica but he'd never gotten around to completing the requisite steps. She was single and an above average looker. Her slightly overweight figure gave him a feeling that she'd be a good partner to play with.

After twenty years his marriage to Terry had grown very tired. Now he was thinking about ending it. He wondered what she was thinking about her desultory existence with him. Her paralegal career was a poor substitute for a loving husband. Sex was only one small missing piece in their life's puzzle. She was still an attractive woman at forty-six and their marriage had been childless. They could part without much complication.

The ice-cold draft beer hit the spot. He and Monica were sitting in a booth away from the crowded bar scene. The Char House was a popular after-work watering hole on Second Avenue, a short walk from the medical clinic building they worked in on First Avenue. The medical/pediatric group they were part of was a close affiliate of the NYU medical school.

They were each working on their second beer and a third wasn't far off. Conversation was mostly about their practice and covered old ground. Halfway through their third Monica suggested they go to her apartment and pick up some Japanese takeout on the way. She knew Bert often ate dinner out before heading home. She also knew his marriage was on life-support. They'd had many friendly conversations at Char House over beers, so she didn't feel guilty about making the offer. She wasn't invading a happy household.

Monica's own situation was uncomplicated. She and her boyfriend had recently parted company on less than friendly terms. She looked forward to male company for dinner this evening. She knew Bert had his eye on her so there'd be more to follow.

Bert knew Terry would be late tonight so this would work out.

Bert was nearing fifty and felt incomplete. His practice was marginally satisfying and was beginning to feel humdrum. For the most part his young patients were in good health and needed very little of his extensive knowledge. When they were very ill he passed the problem on to a consultant specialist. When he imagined doing the same practice for twenty more years he found that prospect decidedly uninspiring.

The unopened takeout grew cold on the kitchen table as he confirmed his suspicion about his and Monica's compatibility. He wondered how this would play out at work. Monica was nearly twenty years his junior so he didn't envision a serious relationship taking root here. On the other hand, they each were looking for what the other was willing to provide.

CHAPTER SIX

Several weeks earlier

O n the cab ride home from work, Bert reflected on his recent visit with his mother, Sophie. Bert had always felt the need to help her gain a measure of revenge for the horror the Nazis had inflicted on their family. Sophie's mother, two sisters, and her older brother, along with a host of other family members, were just ashes scattered at a number of sites outside the gates of Auschwitz and other lesser-known Nazi crematoriums. Her father and younger brother were murdered the day she left Stroudheim, all alone, at thirteen. The recent synagogue massacre pointed him in a decisive new direction, albeit one that wouldn't punish the actual murderers.

He stopped off at Sophie's apartment to deliver some needed groceries. She lived alone in a rent-regulated, one-bedroom apartment in lower Manhattan. Tonight he'd stay for dinner. This gave her great pleasure.

She greeted him at the door with a warm embrace.

"It's so good to see you, Bertie."

"Me too, Mom. Remember, I was here three days ago so it's not as if I'm a stranger to this apartment."

"I know, I know. It's just that I always feel so joyful when I see you. Hang up your jacket and wash up. Tonight I made your favorite, brisket with roasted potatoes."

Bert, her only child, was a late in life baby, born after she escaped the Nazis as a teenager near the end of the war and came to America. He was doted on by his lonely mother. For some reason she had no close friends to pass the time with. He loved her very much and couldn't bear to see her suffer through the anti-Semitic attacks that randomly appeared on the nightly news programs.

After dinner he helped her clean up. Then he sat in the living area and listened to her recall memories of their long-ago decimated family. It was a ritual he'd sat through on countless evenings, after countless briskets.

Her story was indelibly imprinted on his brain. He could recite it with her in unison.

"Bert, a light snow was falling in Stroudheim. January was usually a very busy time in the little town since it sat at the base of a very popular ski mountain. Now, early 1944 was not a time of great festivity for Germans. Most of Europe was under German control, but the news from the eastern front was not encouraging. A great many German casualties were coming home from Russia and this dampened any attempt at winter gaiety."

"Our small family had lived in Stroudheim since fleeing the SS in Dresden two years previous. Our Jewish identity was a closely guarded secret. My parents ran a popular bakery and my two older sisters worked in its kitchen. My younger brother Isaac and I were in school all day. Life seemed to be under control until our Jewish identity was passed along to the local authorities by some hateful townsperson."

"Mom, did you ever learn why this person turned you in after the family had been well-established in the town for over two years?"

"We can only guess, but the hatred for Jews was never far below the surface."

She continued, "My father, mother, and two sisters were not in the bakery when Isaac and I returned home after school. The bakery was boarded up. We ran to our nearby home. On the way we saw our father hanging by the neck from a lamppost. We were too frightened to stop and stare. A friendly neighbor told us to get home, pack quickly, and leave. I knew where my mother hid some money so I quickly emptied that cache and prepared to get away."

"I'm amazed at how you had such presence of mind in those circumstances."

"Before we could escape, a truck drove up to the house and two SS men got out. I went into a prepared hiding place but Isaac was grabbed in the house by an SS officer. He was pulled into the street and shot in the head. The house was searched and my hideout was discovered."

"You had to be terrified, Mom."

"Believe me, Bertie. It was fear like I never knew before. I had no idea what they were going to do with me.

"Each officer took a turn raping me while his partner held me down on a bed. I screamed and cried but it meant nothing to them. When they were finished they threatened me not to leave town and said I should be grateful they were letting me live. They promised to return for a repeat performance.

"After nightfall I went outside to look for my brother. I found his body in the street. Too shocked to cry, I quickly left Stroudheim and set out, at age thirteen, for some place far away."

"I know you had no idea where to go. I'm always amazed by your courage. I don't know how you did it, all alone."

She usually ended the story here. This one day haunted her every day of her life. The tale of her arduous escape to America was oft-repeated as well. As a young boy hearing this story over and over, Bert vowed to do whatever he could someday to give her some measure of revenge against the Nazis. The revenge would be *his* as well since the family tragedy was his inheritance.

Tonight Sophie was focused on the synagogue massacre in Albany. Every atrocity against a Jewish group or gathering triggered the same response. Her anger spilled over into hatred of anything remotely associated with Nazi ideology.

"My darling son, I'm always talking vengeance to you, a man committed to saving lives and caring for people in need. We never seem to spend an evening enjoying what we have, instead of dwelling on what we lost. You're so patient with me, Bertchick. I can't help myself. I feel so guilty for having escaped. I still see my beloved baby brother lying in the street in a pool of his blood."

"I don't mind listening, Mom. Your loss was my loss. I feel it too."

"I pray for retribution. I don't know in what form that vengeance will come, but I'm sure God will not let the Holocaust and today's anti-Semitism go unpunished. I only hope I live to see that day."

Bert heard this as a plea from his mother that *he* should be the avenging angel, even though she never uttered a word to that effect. It left him feeling impotent.

Bert had sat through many sessions like this with Sophie, yet he always shed tears for her. Tonight there was one difference. She looked unwell. He could see evidence of wasting in her face and arms. Her abdomen protruded although this was partially concealed by her loose dress and apron. What alarmed him most though was her color. Her skin was sallow and the whites of her eyes showed evidence of jaundice. The signs were unmistakable. Some form of cancer was far advanced. She was dying and would resist any attempt on his part to have her see a physician. She always did, and not surprisingly, played true-to-form tonight when he tried in vain to get her to agree to see one.

The realization that Sophie's death was fast approaching created in him an urgency to bring her a measure of satisfaction that her hated enemies had paid a price for their crimes. Bitterness was taking control of him.

CHAPTER SEVEN

Still several weeks earlier

Until now Bert always felt like a helpless sufferer who could only share Sophie's anger. Tears wouldn't suffice. He would take on a vengeful role, the one Sophie was praying for. He would answer her prayers, but he would also give his own life new meaning.

A perpetually sorrowful mother with a family to avenge, the void of a fatherless childhood, unanswered anti-Semitic atrocities, a failing marriage and a career he had lost interest in, had all conspired to drive him in a direction he never anticipated.

Behind it all, though, lay an unnatural relationship with a lonely mother. This was buried deep in his subconscious but was operative nevertheless. It fostered a lifelong obsession for revenge that was just waiting to be unleashed.

There were many examples of people taking extreme measures to satisfy a cause they believed in devoutly: kamikaze pilots, human bombs in the Mideast, self-immolation. He had a kinship with these self-sacrificers, with one difference: he would not self-destruct. His was not a one-time event. He would persist as long as the Nazi atrocities continued. It was important that he survive and continue to wage his own war.

An idea had grown in his mind. Life was passing him by and now he saw an opportunity to rescue it. His need for personal safety paled when contrasted with the objective he was adopting.

He believed that Jews were at war with the neo-Nazis but only Jews were paying the ultimate price. He would let the neo-Nazis know that in a war there is a price *both* sides must pay. He carefully planned to execute neo-Nazi leaders. Bert knew it was not his right to take the lives of people who might only profess a Nazi outlook but not actually carry out any violent acts. His rationale was that in a war you eliminated the enemy, even those who carried out menial tasks, and not only the soldiers who perpetrated the killings. The enemy's own personal stories were never considered.

As a respected doctor with no obvious connection to the assassinations, he could carry out his plan and continue his ordinary life. He just had to be extremely careful and not overreach. The actual numbers killed would be small, but the message would eventually become clear to the neo-Nazis: they were going to pay a price for the hate they spewed and the actions it inspired.

Bert had little experience with guns but he was a good learner. He read up on rifles and purchased one through a private sale. The M24 is the standard sniper weapon of the US army. It comes with a telescopic sight and is made by Remington Arms. On weekends he practiced shooting in a deserted wooded area. Rather than joining a gun club where he might be noticed and remembered, he chose to develop the necessary skills on his own. His marksmanship improved to the point where he considered himself highly competent.

Next he needed to develop a roster of targets in the metropolitan New York area. It didn't matter to him where any recent neo-Nazi assault occurred, the retaliation would take place in the New York area unless he had time off and could define some targets elsewhere. That would make his detection much more difficult, but it was a plan that could wait a while.

He purchased publications on a newsstand which seemed to glorify the neo-Nazi ethos. There were a number of far-right, neo-Nazi websites that he culled from Wikipedia. From various sources it was easy to identify likely targets in the area. Then he was ready to act. He waited for an anti-Semitic attack that would serve as his trigger. When the Albany synagogue shooting took place, he decided the time was right to launch his one-man offensive. Gus Oren was an easy target. Bert selected a good place to set up his weapon and waited for Gus to leave work. His marksmanship was lethal. He returned home unnoticed. His weapon was stored under the back seat of his car. He planned to do his shooting from the car whenever possible to avoid being seen carrying the weapon. The gun could be broken down into two pieces if necessary to make it less conspicuous to carry.

Bert considered it essential that he follow a normal lifestyle. That was his cover. He was an inconspicuous pediatrician making a decent living with no political involvement to single him out as a vengeful killer.

He looked the part of a mild-mannered, middle-aged physician. He was an athletic, average-looking six-footer with greying hair at the temples and sideburns. He wore rimless eyeglasses and dressed casually without any affectations. The fact that his marriage was failing didn't single him out as unusual. All in all, he was not likely to attract attention from the police.

CHAPTER EIGHT

When Leslie heard about the murder in the South Bronx she put in a call to Lionel Cobb, the senior homicide detective whose name appeared in the brief newspaper story about the killing. Two neo-Nazi killings within two weeks of the synagogue massacre struck her as an interesting coincidence to look into.

Cobb grudgingly agreed to meet her for lunch. Her angle on the recent killing, coupled with the killing two weeks prior, got his attention.

The Blue Wave diner was convenient for each of them. Cobb did a double-take when Leslie took off her coat and hung it on the coat hook. She was a knockout without seeming to play off it. In a simple skirt and cardigan sweater she drew looks in the diner from men and women. He swallowed hard and rose to greet her.

"I'm pleased to meet you Ms. Nugent." He shook her hand and noticed the absence of a wedding band.

"Likewise, Detective Cobb. I'm glad you were able to make the time for me."

She slid into the booth opposite him and flashed a killer smile.

"If I'd known I was meeting the best-looking reporter from *The Times* I might have picked a more classy spot for lunch. Forgive me, but most of the female reporters I meet don't draw the attention you did when you came in."

"Don't be fooled, Detective. I'm very much the same killer they are. But thanks for the compliment."

"Let's order and then get down to business. One warning, Ms. Nugent. Portions are large here. That's why the cops stop in so often. Their kabobs are pretty good."

"Thanks for the heads-up, Lionel. I hope you don't mind if I call you by your first name; that makes for a more relaxed conversation. Please, call me Leslie."

They ordered and each opted for a draft beer.

Cobb was a large man with an expansive waistline. He was ruddy faced with jowls and red hair turning grey. As a plainclothes detective he wore a blue chambray shirt and striped tie with navy slacks. His grey wool sport-jacket probably dated from a time when he was at least thirty pounds lighter. His clothes looked well cared for. Leslie guessed his age to be around sixty. He had a wedding band on his left hand and no other jewelry.

They talked as they ate. The kabobs were as advertised, well-seasoned and barely fit on the platter they came on.

"I was intrigued by your take on the killing I investigated. The way you put it in your article, Leslie, the two killings could be connected. They each were sniper hits. I won't be surprised if the bullets from the two cases match. If they do, that would go a long way toward your theory that the same sniper did the hits. I'll get the ballistics from the first case and check that out."

"Okay, Lionel, let's say they match and we think there's a killer out there who's knocking off neo-Nazis. Where do we go from there?"

Lionel was making good progress on his kabobs. Leslie was going to have some of her kabobs leftover for a meal tomorrow.

"Let's assume the two murder sites don't offer up any clues, Leslie. You never know. Then we have the gun. Let's assume it's the same gun did the two jobs. Now we have a single killer who has it in for neo-Nazis and is willing to go all the way. What's interesting is the possible connection to the synagogue massacre. That took place far away and it's doubtful either of our victims was connected to that event. If, and it's a *big if*, that's the case, then the killer is just taking revenge and not bothering to target the perps who did the synagogue killings. Makes me think we'll be seeing some more of his or her work in the future."

"Do you bring in the FBI at this point, Lionel, or do you wait until the single shooter theory has legs? For all we know they may already have one eye on this angle and are waiting for more conclusive evidence."

"If they were in on it, I'd know. The FBI doesn't tread lightly, Leslie."

"I guess you check the ballistics, Lionel, and wait and see if more action follows. Two shootings doesn't give us much of a pattern to analyze, although there is the suggestion that the shooter lives in this area."

"One last thing, Leslie. Our conversation is off the record and must be kept private. I need that assurance."

Leslie nodded her assent. They'd exhausted the case material, and now could turn their full attention to the kabobs.

Leslie wondered about Cobb's willingness to share thoughts with a reporter. In her experience and the experience of many other reporters she knew, the police were very close-lipped when discussing cases with the press. She knew that was the traditional police attitude and, in her mind, it was counterproductive. She realized some of her colleagues earned the disrespect of the police, but some of them offered valuable insights and information not to be dismissed out-of-hand. She wondered if Cobb was the exception to that traditional policeman's distrust of the press. His willingness to meet with her gave her hope that they could establish a unique working relationship.

Lionel found Leslie easy to relate to. He was well aware of his colleagues' general attitude toward reporters but he didn't share it. If

THE SNIPER

Leslie turned out to be someone he could trust and share information with then both would be all the richer for the collaboration. He was cautiously willing to stick his neck out and make an effort to find out. Nevertheless, he wouldn't want it spread around the department that he was discussing cases with a member of the press. He was on the cusp of being appointed Chief of Homicide for New York City.

CHAPTER NINE

Bert Alder came home to a darkened apartment. He knew Terry was working tonight so he had supper alone at a Japanese restaurant near his office.

He'd put in a long and tiring day, so having this time to himself was a welcome respite. He poured himself a glass of Black Label over ice and settled into the very comfortable stuffed chair in the living room. He didn't expect Terry home before eleven so he had two hours to reflect on the day's events.

Bert had grown up in a middle-class neighborhood of the Bronx, the only child of Sophie Alder. His mother had little money when she emigrated to the United States from Europe, but a successful uncle in the States was generous and supported her and then Bert when he was born. Bert's biological father parted company from Sophie shortly before Bert was born. He and Sophie had never married and he wasn't interested in starting a family.

THE SNIPER

Sophie saw a succession of men. but true romance never developed. Her mood was too dark for men who were interested in a good time. An occasional male friend of hers found the boy to be an unwanted intruder in the house. Some were even physically violent or abusive toward him when Sophie was not around. Young Bert couldn't defend himself and suffered these assaults in silence.

For her, Bert, her little boy, was the man she loved. They shared a bed in their small apartment until he began to show signs of puberty. In bed she showered her love on the prepubescent boy in ways she knew society frowned upon. She performed oral sex on him and took baths with him up until his early teen years. For him this was his mother's way of showing her love, a love in which he shared equally. After puberty began, the sex briefly became more adult, but this ended as he began to feel an attraction toward girls he met in school. He was terribly conflicted but then his physical relationship with Sophie normalized when he went away to college.

Sophie never alluded to that period of early sexual contact with him. For her it was blotted out from memory. For him it was a hazy part of his childhood that he couldn't or wouldn't examine too closely.

Sophie worked as a salesperson in a large department store. Bert was her life. He was a star student and won a full college scholarship when he graduated from the esteemed Bronx High School of Science. After college at Williams and medical school at Yale, he had trained in pediatrics at NYU. He entered private practice right after completing his training, joining a quality multispecialty group affiliated with Columbia. Shortly after entering practice he married Terry Lofton. His income, combined with Terry's salary as a paralegal, was modest, but they still found it possible to enjoy a comfortable life in New York City.

The one negative in his life was the failure of his marriage to Terry. They had met during his residency when she was just finishing her paralegal training. The chemistry was there but that was all. It wasn't enough. He was solitary and she was social in a friendly, aggressive way. Bert could never make the whole-hearted commitment to Terry that she expected from her husband. She speculated to Bert that he was still tied to his mother with strings she couldn't cut. Terry had genuine affection for Sophie, but saw the bond that enveloped mother and son had kept her walled off from Bert.

Terry and he grew apart and were now each privately wondering how best to end the marriage. She was looking for intimacy and had found it, for the time being, with a senior lawyer in the firm where she worked. Bert had found no substitute for his wife aside from the non-committal, occasional dalliance with Monica. Both he and Monica were aware of the considerable age difference between them. That allowed each to consider their relationship temporary with little prospect of anything more serious developing.

CHAPTER TEN

The Department of Pediatrics had an annual gala for the staff, residents, and large donors. The Alders, Terry and Bert, were a conspicuously handsome couple. Bert was being honored as the department's number one physician fund-raiser. Leslie Nugent was in the crowd as the guest of Doctor Robert Klein, the hospital's newest staff anesthesiologist.

Bert Alder along with Terry approached Leslie and Bob Klein. Bert extended his hand to shake Leslie's and then Bob's. Some light banter followed the introductions but Leslie could feel Bert's eyes on her. Her cocktail dress was quite modest, displaying a minimum of cleavage, yet his eyes hinted at his interest.

Bob was drawn into doctor talk with Bert while Leslie and Terry had a serious conversation about doctors' wives. When the evening ended, Bob and Leslie took a cab to her apartment building. It was too late for him to go upstairs with her so they parted with a friendly kiss. After seeing her safely into her building, he continued on to his address.

Leslie undressed and got into her nightgown, but before putting out her light, she called her close friend, Diane Bowman. Diane was a practicing clinical psychologist. She knew Diane was very likely awake at midnight. She rarely turned in before 1:00 a.m.

"Hey, Diane. I just got back from a big hospital bash. I met some-one who you might know. Terry Alder, the wife of Doctor Bert Alder. When she told me she was a graduate of Sarah Lawrence College I asked if she knew you and she was glad to hear your name. I guess you were a few years behind her at Sarah Lawrence?"

"We were loosely friendly in college but ran in different circles. In recent years we've become close friends, Leslie. What did you think of her?"

"Bright and interesting. A very well-put-together woman. I thought the three of us would hit it off. I'd like to set up a luncheon date if you're agreeable."

"Good suggestion, Les. Go for it."

CHAPTER ELEVEN

A bond rally for Israel was the target for neo-Nazis in San Diego. A car drove into a crowd of people waiting to get into the auditorium. Two women were killed and sixteen people were injured. The driver, a Caucasian male with a swastika tattoo on his left upper arm, escaped before the hired security guards could apprehend him.

The police were investigating it as a hate crime.

Bert Alder saw this as an invitation to strike back. He scanned his list of candidates and picked out two for sanctioning. He was in no hurry to kill them both. The first killing would be close in time to the San Diego event. The second could follow a week or more later.

Earl Graham ran a gun shop in nearby Yonkers. He worked alone and kept the store open late Wednesday evening. He was an easy target. Posters in his storefront window advertised a rally for gun owners, thanking the Supreme Court for affirming the Second Amendment. Other posters singled out the Jew elitists who were trying to convert the United States into a country of dark-skinned immigrants.

Bert felt he had a very worthy target. Wednesday evening, as Graham pulled the gate across the front of his store, he was hit in the neck by two bullets, almost severing his head from his body. Bert knew the recovered shells would match the ones used on his previous victims but he didn't care. His message would eventually get out and that was all that mattered. He drove away from the deserted street and headed home satisfied.

CHAPTER TWELVE

Howard Marcus was uncomfortable contemplating a blind date. He was divorced for nearly five years and had been 'fixed-up' often in the first few years after the divorce. Recently, fewer and fewer women were sent his way. The many failed 'hookups' had taken their toll. His referring friends and relatives came to see him as either not interested or just unwilling to go the extra distance needed to make a date into something more than a polite meal or theatre experience.

Tonight he'd accepted a date sent to him by a close friend, anesthesiologist Bob Klein. Bob was a good friend of Leslie Nugent and harbored no unrealistic romantic notions about her. He wished it was otherwise but knew it wasn't to be. Now he was passing her on to a longtime friend whom he respected. He knew all about Howard's dating record. If anyone could bring him back from the depths of dating failure it would be Leslie. Bob had not shared Howard's dismal dating history with her.

They were meeting tonight, never having even glimpsed the other, but with available online résumés. O'Shea's pub in Chelsea was a good place to start. It was unpretentious but the food was inventive and well-prepared. The beer selection was excellent. She'd indicated that beer was high on her list of friendly evening starters. He liked that.

Howard picked her out easily since she sat alone in a booth with a bottle of Blue Moon half emptied into a glass. He slid in opposite her before she could get up to greet him.

"Howard Marcus, Leslie. Nice to meet you." They shook hands across the table, careful not to knock over her beer.

"And I'm Leslie Nugent, Howard. I've never been here before and can see why you picked this place. It's friendly with a warm feel. I like it already and have only had three beers." She put up her hands in mock surrender. "I'm kidding about the beers. This is my first." She flashed a smile and he was already glad he'd made the date.

Howard was a nice looking guy with black wavy hair and brown eyes. He had a youthful look and a lean figure. He was wearing a crewneck sweater over a grey striped shirt. All in all, he made a good first impression. She knew he was forty-five years old and five years divorced without children.

Howard had been pleased with first impressions before and was usually let down in subsequent conversation. In this case, Leslie would have to come down a long way to disappoint him. She was so good to look at.

"Leslie, I'm gonna have a brew and get you a second one if you're ready. Then we can dig into each other's past for some basic bio stuff. You know I'm a psychiatrist at Columbia and I know you're a reporter at *The Times*. I'm five years divorced and you're new to New York. Never married. That's all I've got."

The waitress came over, took their drink orders and left two menus.

"My turn to show how much I know, Howard. Bob gave me some lowdown on you but it wasn't much. You're a psychiatrist, trained at

Harvard. You're a native of Massachusetts who did his college and med school at Yale. That's my entire book on Howard Marcus. Your turn. This is an interesting reversal of form with the two of us spilling the beans about the other."

"My turn, Les. You came here from the D.C. area where you were a news reporter for several years. A big story about the White House got you to *The Times*. You're a Long Island girl even though you've been away for much of your adult life. That's not a lot of background, but I'd like more."

"I don't date a lot, Howard. I've made a lot of friends in New York, male and female, but I'm not romantically involved now. I love my job. Trying to ferret out stories is a real challenge but this city is rich in material."

"I don't know if I could be the source of any material, but if you see an opening where I can be of any use, give me a chance."

"What I know about doctors and hospitals is limited to what I see on the tube and read in an occasional novel. If you come across any homicidal patients or zombie doctors, ring me up. I'm a quick study and can build a story out of very little if given a lead."

"You're on."

The evening was a success on all fronts. The food was surprisingly fine and they each found the other to be an attentive listener. Leslie related some of her recent stories and even touched lightly on her failed romances with distant guys. Howard was easy to talk to and seemed genuinely interested in her private life. He was honest about his failed marriage, sharing the blame with his ex. He admitted it had been a poor match that only became more apparent as time passed. Now he was cautious where romancing women was concerned. The talk was more intimate than one would expect on a first date but each had disarmed the other and let their real selves show, albeit with some holdback.

They split the bill and took a walk through the Village. It was a mild fall evening, just perfect for walking and talking. They held hands as they walked, which each took as an indication that they were likely to see each other again. They Ubered to her apartment building where he let her out, kept the Uber, gently kissed her on the lips, and waited until she was safely inside.

For each it had been a perfect evening. They parted thinking "second date" and feeling something special had taken place.

CHAPTER THIRTEEN

If Howard didn't call by 7:00 p.m., Leslie had made up her mind to make the call. She couldn't believe he didn't feel the same attraction she did. It was only two days after they'd met and still no call. Not even a call to say what a great time he'd had.

The phone ringing interrupted her anxious ruminations.

"Hi, Leslie. You probably wondered why I hadn't called sooner. I apologize. I was caught up in a complex family squabble involving one of my patients and wasn't thinking about anything else. That's over now so I've come back to earth and want to see you as soon as you're available. Like maybe tonight."

"Howard, I'd love to see you. How about La Alhambra on Charles Street in the village at nine?"

"You're on. And you do forgive me for the late call? Just say yes, Leslie."

"Yes, I do forgive you. And you forgive me for any not nice thoughts I might have conjured up while waiting for that call. Okay? That's an even trade. See you in a few hours."

They waited on the street outside La Alhambra for half an hour but the paella was worth it. They emptied two flasks of Sangria that made the conversation flow even easier. The mood of two nights ago hadn't been lost. They were enjoying each other's company better than they had with anyone either had dated in recent memory.

Having gotten past the awkward getting-to-know-you stage, they were talking about their daily lives. Leslie was writing a story about police attitudes toward blacks and how they put stock in how black young men dressed.

"It superficial, Howard, but it's very real. I've talked to a large number of street cops and brass. They seem to be saying to young blacks 'If you dress and talk white you'll get a better shake from the cops.' For the blacks it's an attack on their very culture. The two groups don't seem to know how to bridge the gap. I'm going to talk to some cultural psy-chologists at Columbia. I find this type of work very compelling."

"I can see why, Les. It's real life and you're helping to define an important issue that's at the root of our racial fissure."

"'Racial fissure.' I like that, Howard. May I use it without attrib-ution?"

"It's yours Leslie. Enjoy."

Howard moved on to his own day's experience.

CHAPTER FOURTEEN

FedEx delivered the divorce papers to Bert Alder in his office. He and Terry had agreed that the marriage was a dead end and that they'd be better off parting company. The settlement wouldn't be difficult since they were in general agreement about the divorce and had little property.

He tried to put this matter out of his mind. Tonight he would take out his second victim since the bond rally attack. Wes Glover was a FedEx driver, recently unemployed after his truck collided with a car and the investigating policeman smelled alcohol on his breath.

Bert had run an evening surveillance watch on Glover for the past week and now waited patiently in his car, hoping Glover would follow his usual pattern and show up alone at Monaghan's Bar near the Bronx Zoo around 8:00 p.m. He was parked far down the block with a good view of the bar's entrance. He would take Glover out as he prepared to enter the bar. The street was relatively quiet at night since most stores in the area were closed after six.

Glover was a regular at meetings of the local "Veterans for a Pure America."

He wrote frequent letters to the local newspapers decrying the pollution of the population by blacks and the influence of Jewish money in getting politicians elected who were radical Zionists. He always signed his letters with his name above the title, "Co-Chairman, VPA."

Sure enough, at 8:15 p.m., Glover's noisy Subaru drove up and parked in a spot across the street from Monaghan's. Bert watched him in his telescopic sight and put him down with one headshot as he prepared to cross the street. *It was a good kill,* he thought. He waited a minute or so before slowly driving away. This made his movement a less obvious connection to the shooting if anyone happened to witness the act.

Coming out of the movie theatre with Howard, Leslie's cellphone rang. "Detective Lionel Cobb, Ms. Nugent, homicide. We spoke not long ago about some killings that had a curious similarity. I'm calling to give you a heads-up about a shooting tonight that seems to fit that same mold. There was one a few days ago that may also tie in. I thought you and I should get together again and see if these cases move us any closer to formulating a strategy to catch the sniper, assuming there's only one sniper involved."

"I appreciate your call, Lionel. Thanks for keeping me in the loop. Just tell me when and where we can meet and I'll be there."

CHAPTER FIFTEEN

Leslie met Detective Cobb in his office on a sunny, Sunday morning. The precinct was quiet at this time but not deserted. Cobb was out of uniform, wearing a dark blue flannel shirt and chino slacks. Leslie had also dressed down in running pants and a New York Yankees sweatshirt over a yellow polo shirt with a collar

"I'll be brief, Leslie. You recall our last conversation. Two killings smelled like hate crimes in reverse. Well, the recent two have the same scent. You probably recall the Jewish bond rally in San Diego where a car ran down a number of people and killed two. Very soon after we have two more killings on our hands. They have the same features as the first two. The victims were men and both were involved in neo-Nazi activities. Again, neither seemed to have had a direct hand in the San Diego killings. Both were victims of a sniper and the bullets we found suggest the same gun was used in all four killings."

"Incredible, Lionel. We seem to have a serial killer who has marked neo-Nazis for death. It sure sounds like revenge. Trouble is he or she is very clever and doesn't leave any clues."

"I'm going to access a police profiler, Leslie, to see if we can develop a working model of the sniper. I'm sure you've been trying to do that on your own. I'd be interested in seeing how your model and that of the profiler agree or disagree."

CHAPTER SIXTEEN

L eslie looked forward to her regularly scheduled meeting with her editor, John Livingstone. He was always helpful, offering advice on stories she was working on and potential leads on new stories. His small office belied the regard he was held in at the paper. As usual, every surface above the floor was covered with stacks of paper and books. She cleared off one of the two chairs and sat down.

Today he was very supportive of the neo-Nazi storyline she was pursuing.

"I've got a piece of news to share with you, Leslie. We've hired a new reporter from the West Coast. Hired him away from the *LA Times* and sunny Los Angeles. His name is Gary Hoffman and he specializes in stories with a Jewish angle. I think he'd be an asset working with you on this Nazi story. I know you're worried he'll steal your ideas. Don't worry. You both work for me and I'll keep him honest. I think he's a straight shooter and wouldn't like to think we were questioning his reporter's ethics."

"John, I know you mean well, but I've never worked with a partner on a story. I'm not sure it's a good idea."

"Leslie, he's a real asset. Trust me. He's also single and thirty-eight."

"Okay, Cupid. I'll look him up and get back to you on the partnership once I've sized him up for myself."

The switchboard operator gave her the phone extension number of Gary. She made the call and sat back in her cubicle's desk chair. The call was picked up on the second ring.

"Gary here," was the quick opening response.

"I'm Leslie Nugent, Gary, a colleague of yours here at the paper. John Livingstone suggested I give you a call. He thinks you might be able to help me on a story I'm beginning to develop. I think we could best discuss this in person, Mr. Hoffman."

"Not if you insist on calling me by my father's name. Call me Gary and I'll buy you a coffee in the employee lounge at three. Is it okay if I call you Leslie, Leslie?"

"For a free coffee in the lounge how could a girl resist? See you there in twenty minutes, Gary."

The lounge was nearly empty at three so Leslie had no trouble picking out Gary, seated on one of the sofas.

Leslie saw a rather cute guy with long, black curly hair not combed in any particular style. Or maybe just not combed. He wore a blue button-down shirt slightly frayed at the collar and brown corduroy jeans with creases consistent with many hours at a keyboard. Leslie was quick to note the absence of any jewelry on his left hand. The overall impression was that he cared little about his presentation. Or maybe he did, and this was it. His face was friendly enough though, and actually he was carelessly handsome. He reminded her of the actor Mark Ruffalo.

"Let me get you a coffee, Leslie. That was the enticement and I'm not letting go of you without hearing about the interesting story you lured me with. I bet you take it black."

"Wow. You really nailed me on that one. Am I that obvious about my coffee preference? Kills all sense of mystery about me."

"I'm just a good judge of those things that say a lot about a person, Leslie."

"Enough with the banter, Gary. Let's have that coffee and I'll tell you the story I used to 'lure' you here. A sniper has killed four men in this area who held strong neo-Nazi leanings, two each after distant fatal attacks on Jewish gatherings. The victims were not in the vicinity of the killings as far as we can tell. I think the sniper believes the vics are part of a loosely configured 'army' that's declared war on the Jewish population. He may be waging a one-man war in return. Our only lead is that the killer is probably in the metro New York area because that's where his victims resided. That's essentially it. Oh, one other thing: bullets recovered at each killing site appear to have been fired from the same gun."

"Well, it is an interesting angle. Have you seen *Death Wish* with Charles Bronson? Has some of the same features. Vigilante justice exercised because the standard justice system will only go after the actual perpetrators of crime. This vigilante seems ready to hit the enemy soldiers even if they only exist outside the actual battlefield. That's much the same as the neo-Nazis killing Jews who have little or nothing to do with West Bank settlements or harshly subduing crowds of rock throwing Palestinians. Two sides of the same coin. What's interesting to me is that this seems to be the work of one man. It's not the B'na Brith or the Jewish Alliance taking up arms."

"I can see why John sent me to you. Didn't take much to turn up your burners."

"Leslie, I'm Jewish but don't own a gun. I was born in America and have always lived here. I'm not a Zionist. I do recognize that when the Jewish state was carved out of Palestine it was not anticipated that the displaced Arabs would resist for over seventy years, and that the Jews

43

would not be able to find an accommodation with them. That said, our vigilante is unwilling to give neo-Nazis a free pass. My concern is simple. This person will feed off his success and may eventually seek out others he can trust to form a little army and up the ante. That would be his undoing because a group of one is easy to keep secret. As it expands it will spring some leaks and eventually be eradicated. The neo-Nazis will survive."

"Well put, Gary. You may be right, but this guy is clever and may not adhere to your scenario. He may stay solo, keep killing and satisfy his personal need. I'm not a person who likes to predict the future. I like to play in the present. What I'm looking for is a way to build a story that has legs. I think he will kill again and that will keep my story alive. I also want to solve the mystery of who is doing this killing and what got him started. I know the police and probably the FBI are in this game, but we can out-think them and get closer to the killer sooner than they will. Are you interested, Gary?"

"Yeah, I guess so. It's kind of an offbeat challenge. And I like that. I'm in only on one condition."

"I'm listening, Gary."

"You have dinner with me tomorrow night. What do you say? Dinner at eight, tomorrow night. I'll meet you at your apartment and we can cab to a nice little French bistro I know on Second Avenue."

Leslie didn't miss a beat. He was bright, good looking in a shaggy way, seemingly available and a bit taken with her.

"You're on, Gary. My home address is on the back of this business card."

She handed him the card. "Now that you can see where I live, maybe it would make more sense for me to meet you at the restaurant. I'll leave that up to you. Tell me what works best. I don't know where you live."

"A woman of the world." He glanced at the card. "Let's meet at the restaurant."

After they parted, Leslie walked back to her office with a smile on her face. She'd have to thank John for the referral.

CHAPTER SEVENTEEN

A few weeks later, in the absence of any recent high profile killing of Jews, Bert felt the need to go out and do some hunting anyway. He had plenty of names to choose from. Elgin Block lived on Staten Island and was the owner of several small supermarkets on the island borough.

He went to his car in a nearby garage and soon found himself on the Verrazano Bridge on his way to Staten Island. It was early evening and he planned to do his sniping later into the night. He had scouted Block's routine. Tonight was cards at the house of some old friends. He followed his quarry to the friend's house and parked several blocks away. The terrain was somewhat rough. Even though this was New York City, Staten Island still had areas where nice homes abutted unfinished lots awaiting development. He selected an area in a lot where he could relax for a while and check out his weapon.

The hours passed and around eleven, the card game apparently broke up. Men began to leave. Bert had a good image of Block in his head. He was walking with another man toward his car. It appeared that Block was going to give the other man a ride. This disturbed Bert's simple scenario but didn't deter him. He took aim and fired at Elgin just as he was unlocking his car door. The shot was on target and he fell to the ground like a puppet whose strings had been cut.

Suddenly the other man pulled a gun and was searching the landscape for the shooter. Bert wasted no time. The armed stranger took cover on the wrong side of the car and was easily taken care of with two shots to the torso.

Bert slowly headed away from the scene in a very low crouch. He reached his parked car far across the lot on the opposite side from the victims. He slowly drove away as police sirens were heard and soon passed by him going in the opposite direction. He was many blocks away on the highway leading away from the Verrazano Bridge by the time the police determined what had happened. He headed into New Jersey to avoid cameras on the bridge tollbooths going into Brooklyn. He figured the police would review the tapes for the hour following the shooting and look for matches going into Staten Island in the hours preceding the shooting. He didn't know what they'd look for, but he didn't want to be a part of that review. He'd reenter Manhattan through the Lincoln Tunnel.

He wondered who his second victim was. He had no remorse. In his wartime scenario, collateral damage could not be avoided.

CHAPTER EIGHTEEN

Lionel Cobb called Leslie with the news. "There was a shooting tonight on Staten Island with some hallmarks of the previous four killings. A sniper shooting and a neo-Nazi victim. Several differences though. No recent attack on Jews and this time our shooter encountered *two* men. He killed them both. The second man was not connected to the neo-Nazis in any way we could determine. He was collateral damage. Trouble is he was a senior police officer on the Staten Island force. As you might imagine, the SI police are enraged."

"I wish I had some new insights, Lionel. I've been working on another story while this one seemed dormant. What did the profiler have to offer?"

"Not much we hadn't already figured out ourselves. There just aren't any clues. We keep hoping for some chance sighting by a passerby. No such luck."

"Lionel, something has changed. He grew impatient waiting for an attack on Jews. He seems to have escalated to killing without a fresh provocation. It shows he may be growing content to kill the enemy whenever he feels the need. I have a colleague at the paper who is going to be working with me on this story. He's very bright and may help us form a plan to smoke out this very clever sniper."

"One last thing, Leslie. The profiler I consulted had nothing to offer that we hadn't already put on the table. It was reassuring, though, to have someone distant from the case come up with a similar analysis. The profiler saw a middle-aged male, educated, with a significant loss, seeking vengeance. Considering his targets, she didn't think it was a far stretch that he was possibly Jewish with some tie-in to the Holocaust. The recent atrocities triggered a long brewing hostility but were experienced on a background of other perceived unhappy circumstances. The sniper had more than one trigger in his life to explain why he was acting at this time. That's what she offered. Sounded reasonable to me.

"Forgive my gallows humor, Leslie, but we're now going to round up all the educated, middle-aged Jewish males in New York and bring them in for questioning."

CHAPTER NINETEEN

Gary and Leslie stopped at a lunch cart on the walkway just outside Central Park

"I've got some news, Leslie. I met with some people I know in the local leadership of Jewish organizations. I wanted to hear their take on the sniper killings you've covered so well in your columns."

"Good angle, Gary. I like it."

"Well, no surprise. They're keeping their hands off the matter. Without saying as much, they agreed that killing is wrong but in this case they were taking some satisfaction in the sniper's selection of targets. I think they see him as heroic, in a sense. He's doing what we might wish more had the courage to do. They're not encouraging others to join in and start an all-out war with the neo-Nazis. On this one-man scale, it has the effect of allowing the Jewish leaders to stand back and publicly neither condemn nor cheer on the shooter. I found the meeting stimulating. I was sorry you weren't there to hear it yourself. Next time I see an opening in the story I'll certainly call you in."

"I hope so, Gary, and vice versa. What did they think was going to happen in the short term?"

"They think he'll continue to do more of the same. One opinion emerged. They believe that anyone willing to go this far must have a mighty grudge. They'd tie it back to a very tragic family loss. The Holocaust offers that kind of tragic loss for many Jews, or the recent synagogue killings."

"That's all helpful, Gary, but we shouldn't lose sight that Jews aren't the only people who have great disdain for the neo-Nazis. I think they'd be number one, though, when it comes to taking such extreme measures of revenge."

"You're right, Leslie. But my bet is still on a vengeful Jewish male."

"I think we're very much in agreement on that, Gary. Getting back to your meeting with Jewish leaders, you've written a great sidebar for my next column. Only thing missing is a similar meeting with neo-Nazi leaders. I'd like to hear *their* take on this. I suspect they'd hide behind their First Amendment rights and consider the sniper a deranged homicidal maniac. We should meet with those brown shirts."

"I think you're right on target, Leslie. I wonder how their leaders are reacting. After all, the sniper has made it clear that *they* are his targets. It's one thing to speak from a protected podium; it's another to lead a normal life wondering if a sniper has you in his sights. I think the sniper has a clear goal: intimidate the leadership and see if that mutes the organization's aggressive behavior."

"I have a contact at the local FBI office, Gary, and she might be able to get us in contact with some leadership guys in the local neo-Nazi organization."

"Keep me in the loop, Leslie. Let's move together on this. I couldn't ask for a better excuse to ask you out."

"You don't need an excuse, Gary, even if we don't have any new work-related issues to discuss."

CHAPTER TWENTY

The apartment was much smaller than the one he and Terry had lived in together. Bert now had big expenses as a consequence of the divorce and didn't need a large condo. This one was a modest one-bedroom in an eighty-year-old building in the Upper West Side just off Amsterdam Avenue. Not shabby but not modern inside. It was just below street level with its own private entrance. Best of all, it was just a short walk to the subway and not far from Lincoln Center.

Since the shooting on Staten Island he'd been laying low.

Leslie's stories in *The Times* were right on target but were missing one crucial piece. She had no idea who the sniper was. Bert Alder was determined not to yield to temptation and seek her out socially. He remembered her at the hospital bash and was drawn toward her. It was tempting to meet her and get into a discussion of the theories being put forward in her articles. That might be a way to impress her. *Bad idea*, he

51

cautioned himself, *keep away from any discussion of the sniper*. Maybe seeking her out was a foolish idea. He decided to avoid such risky behavior.

CHAPTER TWENTY-ONE

This was her first visit to Gary's apartment. Without seeing it she could have described it pretty well. It was well-organized clutter. It was Gary. There was no concern for style, but that was him. He was consistent. Everywhere she looked there were books, newspapers, or magazines. A few family photos managed to secure a place atop the dresser in his bedroom. He pointed out his mother and father and a sister with two children. There was nothing unusual about his family that she could discern from the pictures. A New York Mets poster was taped to the wall next to the bed. The single bed was loosely 'made' with no bedspread. The kitchen was clean and, to her surprise, there were no dishes in the sink. A look in the refrigerator explained the empty sink; there was scarcely any food in the fridge or freezer. Gary obviously did little cooking at home.

Leslie took this all in with one quick tour of the apartment. She took a seat on the lone chair in the living area and Gary plunked himself down on the worn sofa.

"Okay, Leslie, you look like you want to start the conversation. Out with it."

"My FBI contact was helpful after I explained the reason for my request. She offered me a list of names. Some were on special watch because they were considered dangerous and had been questioned in connection with violent activities in the past. I asked her to identify any people she'd call leaders. At this point she became cautious and wanted to know if I was planning on feeding the names to the sniper. She was serious. I had to convince her of my good intentions. I must have succeeded because she released the names to me of those she considered leaders."

"Leslie, just hope that no one on the list is bumped off by the sniper in coming days. That would earn you a place on the FBI watch list as a possible confederate of the sniper. No joke, Leslie. You've put yourself in a curious position where law enforcement is concerned."

"I understand, Gary. Too late to change that. Now let's plan a meeting with some of these 'brown shirts.' I'll call a few names on the list and see if I can set up a group meeting with five or six of the brass. Once the meeting is set up we'll have to think about how we approach these guys. What's their level of concern?"

"I'd bet they're very concerned, Les, now that five of their number have been offed by the sniper. The question is how they're going to respond. The FBI isn't sure what to do. They have little experience in a civil war like this. Are they going to offer the neo-Nazis protection? And can they really protect them? The president has refrained from offering his two cents. I think he'll eventually come out against murder and avoid the obvious revenge motivation guiding the sniper."

"You're probably right, Gary. The sniper is clever though. He has no timetable. The FBI may try to put a protective shield over the Nazis, but will grow tired of that when there are no more killings. They can take undeserved credit and back away if the sniper lays low for a while. And *who* will the FBI try to protect? How many Nazis? They're in a tight spot."

"And will the Nazis accept protection? Leslie, it makes them look weak. One sniper, presumably Jewish, is terrorizing the neo-Nazi leadership. This is a conundrum for all involved except the sniper. And two reporters."

Gary held up one finger, signaling an additional thought.

"One last thought, Leslie. The Nazis may find this to be justification for a sniper of their own. Meet the supposed Jewish sniper head on and hunt him down. The Nazis can't let the shootings go on without a response on their part."

"I agree there will have to be a response. They can't afford to look docile in the face of a one-man Jewish threat. I think they'll take some action but I haven't the foggiest what it will be. I'll bet there's real concern in the 'fatherland.'"

"Leslie, I think it's time to call it quits and have that dinner we planned for tonight. Let's grab our coats and move out. We can continue this discussion after our pre-dinner drinks arrive."

CHAPTER TWENTY-TWO

Americans for America was part of a loosely connected network of neo-Nazi organizations across the United States. There was no centralized leadership in the country. Numerous small groups espousing support for the neo-Nazi cause were unified by their common belief in the Nazi program. Publications repeatedly stated the Nazis' goals and, even without top-down leadership, gave these small organizations a sense of belonging to a larger one, even though it only existed as a common belief system.

Local cells elected their leaders and met on a quasi-regular basis to swear allegiance to the Nazi cause. An occasional action was launched to disrupt their common enemy's planned activities. There was no coordinated effort among locals. Actions were sporadic and widely dispersed. The most detested enemy was any Jewish organization, although black and brown Americans were fast approaching the Jews as a most hated enemy.

Leslie called the first name on her list of presumed neo-Nazi leaders.

"Hello, this is Herman Midler, how can I help you?"

"Mr. Midler, I'm Leslie Nugent, a *New York Times* reporter. I've been covering the recent sniper shootings. You may have seen some of my stories in the paper. I'm trying to set up a meeting with some people who the sniper may identify as sharing beliefs that tie together his victims."

"Stop dancing around the point, Ms. Nugent. You want to talk about the sniper with some people who espouse the neo-Nazi cause. Is that it?"

"Yes, Mr. Midler. I'd like to meet with you and perhaps five of your colleagues to discuss the sniper matter. I'd prefer that your colleagues be people in leadership positions. I have a list of names. Perhaps we could go down the list and identify five colleagues to invite to an informal session at a site of your choosing."

"I can see what's in it for you. What's in it for my people?"

"Good question, Mr. Midler. You'd have an opportunity to share your ideas with your peers and possibly come up with a strategy to respond to the situation. You don't need me for that. I might be able to articulate your response so that your position would be understood by the public. You might even engender sympathy. Of course, I'd have to hear that position."

"You sound like a very clever woman, Ms. Nugent. Are you a Jew?"

"Just so happens, I'm not." Leslie decided not to pursue this angle any further.

"What do you say, Mr. Midler? Think we can put this meeting together?"

"I'll give it some thought and get back to you."

"Okay, here's my cellphone number. I hope to hear from you."

CHAPTER TWENTY-THREE

Fortunately for Leslie, Howard Marcus had been out of town attending a medical meeting in Chicago for the past week. She hadn't figured out how to juggle her time between Howard and Gary. Now Howard was back in New York and the messages on her phone indicated that he was as eager to see her as he was when they last were together.

Given her intense work schedule, the best she could arrange was a lunch date. He was disappointed but understood her bind. Now they sat face to face in a busy soup-and-salad place in Midtown. Fortunately, it was after the noon rush, so the place was beginning to quiet down and allow them to eat at a leisurely pace while they talked. No one was haunting their table encouraging them to get up and leave.

Leslie soon realized her feelings for him were unchanged. He made her feel at ease. She knew they had real potential as a couple. The only problem was Gary. Eventually, one of the guys would have to be consigned to second place. Right now she wasn't ready to make that decision.

The conversation couldn't avoid the sniper story Leslie was pursuing with great intensity. Howard offered some valuable insights from the psychiatric point of view.

"The sniper isn't some unhinged killer. He's very purposeful, extremely careful and very patient. These are the hallmarks of a mature, intelligent person. He could hold down a responsible position. He's not at loose ends. If he was, he might be expected to take some irrational steps. He is a killer, though, and that can't be set aside.

"Having said all that, there is some experience in his past that leaves him vulnerable to seeking out a violent solution to his problem. Something has now triggered that lurking propensity in him. If he were my patient I'd try to understand *why* he has taken on this cause *at this time*. What has pushed him into this messianic role at this moment in his life. Once the patient reveals this I'd know a lot about him and could try to guide him out of the vengeful mode he's in. Hey, I'm lecturing and haven't given you an opportunity to fire back."

"I'm all ears, Howard. I agree with your analysis but don't see us getting any closer to identifying the shooter. Can you think of any way we can reach out to him and possibly establish a line of communication?"

"Let's think a minute, Les. The communication could be through you and your paper. That's one side of the communication line. He may read it. Then the question is whether he'd respond. I think he might. He's probably looking for a way to state his position, not for sympathy, but rather to gain support or understanding for his justification. He doesn't need anyone's help and he's not recruiting acolytes. Remember, he's smart. An understanding public would be less likely to help the authorities catch him. Also, he may be dying to talk."

"So you think I should print an open letter to the sniper and see if he responds. There's nothing to lose. I just don't want the paper to appear to be condoning his killings."

"I'm sure you can manage a way to be, at worst, neutral. Let me read the 'letter' before you send it out. I may have some ideas."

CHAPTER TWENTY-FOUR

The two reporters agreed that some grunt work might prove helpful. They decided to develop a list of known Holocaust survivors living in the New York area. That was not going to reveal the sniper's identity but might serve as useful to cross-reference with some other piece of related data if they were clever or lucky enough to unearth anything relevant. So far they had very little to work on. This was a far reach but the sniper, him or herself, might be a relative of the survivor. It was a place to go so they set about obtaining the names.

A list of registered gun owners in the same area might also be useful, recognizing that many guns are not registered. Still, it was worth having in hand. Cross-referenced with the survivors, this would be a start.

Lionel Cobb had indicated that the shooter was a skilled marksman so Leslie also developed a list of gun clubs in the area. Using her best persuasive skills, she was able to get a list of gun club members from most of the clubs. This was another list to cross-reference. She also would keep military experience as another aspect to examine, but wasn't sure how to get that information.

Gary suggested they arbitrarily try to identify Jewish males on any list they assembled. This was not simple but he believed in doing the best you can, as opposed to doing nothing. It might be illusory, but they had nothing to lose. They pulled in a couple of newspaper interns to help with the work. John Livingstone was kept abreast of what they were doing and gave it his blessing.

One consequence of this labor was that it kept Leslie and Gary in close contact every day. Their relationship was beginning to mature and they found themselves frequently spending evenings in each other's apartments.

Gary seemed so right for her. She saw that two reporters would have no difficulty understanding each other's career goals and daily work objectives. Always looming was the danger that one or the other might receive a job offer in some distant city and plunge them into a long-distance relationship. Gary had in fact recently made such a move from Los Angeles as she had from Washington. In addition, she saw them as potential competitors seeking advancement at the same employer.

She realized that she was gun-shy when it came to a distant courtship. That had proven fatal to her two previous brushes with a permanent relationship. Recently she learned that Howard was being looked at by several leading academic centers for a department chairmanship position. One was on the West Coast and the other in Texas. A bit disconcerting for her.

All in all, Gary seemed the right guy for her. His natural warmth, good humor, and relaxed approach to life were very appealing. Now she needed to know if he felt similarly about her. So far they had been very good friends, but there had been no physical intimacy. She was ready to see that change.

It would have pleased Leslie to know that Gary's mind was taking the same turn. He saw the need to heat up their relationship and find out if they would be as close physically as they were emotionally and intellectually. This made sense if they saw themselves as having a future together.

CHAPTER TWENTY-FIVE

Waiting for Midler to call back was making Leslie tense and disagreeable. Gary could sense her anxiety and knew the reason for it. He tried to shake her loose of it by suggesting a variety of activities, none of which appealed to her. For the moment, she was out of reach. He decided to give her all the space she needed.

Midler wasn't sitting idle trying to decide what to do. He called a meeting of his council leadership and posed the option to them. All six men agreed the meeting with a resultant article in *The Times* could be useful. If managed properly, they could come away with public sympathy and use the coverage to explain their point of view on several issues to *The Times'* left-wing readership. They could see no downside and told Midler to set up the meeting.

Leslie's cell phone broke her moment of reverie. She answered before the second ring. Midler was agreeable to having the meeting she proposed. He offered his house for the meeting and gave her a few agreeable dates and times. They quickly agreed on the logistics. Leslie indicated her desire to bring along a fellow reporter. She was pleased to hear him easily agree to the inclusion. She chose not to tell Midler that her colleague was Jewish.

Two nights later Leslie and Gary found themselves in a residential section of the Bronx that neither had visited before. The houses here were mostly attached, two-family units. The tree-lined streets were free of rubbish and the trees were seemingly well cared for. It had the look of a working class neighborhood with everyone employed and bringing home a good paycheck.

They left the car and easily identified the address Midler had given.

"So far, so good, Les. Aren't you glad I left my Star of David back in the apartment?"

She smiled faintly.

"Okay. We're there. Ring the bell."

The door was opened by a pleasant-looking woman wearing slacks and a sweater under a simple apron. Leslie gauged her to be in her late forties.

"Hello, I'm Bernice Midler. Welcome to my house. Come on in. Herman and the men are all here and waiting for you in the living room. There's coffee and cake on the table along the wall so I hope you'll help yourself. The men have had a head-start on the refreshments."

Bernice ushered the two of them into a large living room where six men were sitting in no particular arranged order. Two empty chairs were obviously for them and were situated to place the reporters facing the men. They all rose as Leslie and Gary entered and one of them came forward and introduced himself as Herman Midler.

Leslie had envisioned Midler as a ruddy Germanic type, so she was surprised to find herself shaking hands with a wiry, balding man only a few inches taller than her five foot six height. She introduced Gary and Midler shook his hand. The host indicated the coffee and food his wife had laid out. They each took a cup of coffee and a piece of strudel and sat down in their appointed chairs.

"Let me first introduce the men in the room." Midler then went around the room, naming the men and indicating their occupations. Leslie wrote their names down in her notebook and noted their positions in the room.

"And I'm Herman Midler. I work at Sutton Motors, a Ford dealership. I manage the accounts at Sutton. I'm a CPA." He paused and Leslie took the opportunity to introduce herself and Gary to the group.

"I'm Leslie Nugent and this is Gary Hoffman. We're both general news reporters at *The Times* and each have over ten years of reporting experience. I'll cut to the chase. I think you know that Gary and I have been covering the sniper story. We felt it would be helpful to hear from people with views not dissimilar from the five victims the sniper has chosen to kill. Our investigations suggest that you men could be targets for the sniper. I hope you'll forgive me for making assumptions about you that may be wrong. We're here to learn about your take on the sniper matter. We hope you'll be candid with us."

Midler stood up and asked the reporters to start off the questions. Gary felt it incumbent to speak and stood up.

"Leslie and I decided not to structure this discussion. We want to hear what's on your minds and not bend the session to meet our preconceived notions."

The room was silent. One man among the six facing the reporters stood up and identified himself. "I'm Arnold Haas. I own a food market in this neighborhood. My take on the sniper is that he's a person with a grudge who has become deranged."

Leslie picked up on that opening. "Thank you, Mr. Haas. What do you think his grudge is about and how is he selecting his targets?"

Haas paused but a moment to formulate his response. "He hates white Christians and picks out those who he thinks hold strong views about Jews and foreigners."

Gary stepped in here. "Thanks for starting us off, Mr. Haas. I guess you believe the shooter is not a 'white Christian' and disagrees with your opinion about 'Jews and foreigners.'"

"Let's not dance around the issue here, Mr. Hoffman. It seems obvious he's a disgruntled Jew. He's picking victims he believes to be Nazi sympathizers based on what he reads in the papers."

Gary stayed on this tack. "Has he been wrong in the selection of victims, Mr. Haas?" He turned to the broader audience. "Are any of you Nazi sympathizers?"

Another man stood up and identified himself. "I'm Richard Vogel. I'm the owner and editor of an America for Americans newspaper. I think Arnold has said what all of us are thinking. Thank you, Arnie. My newspaper is a popular voice in this community. We're not Nazis but we find much to admire in the Nazi philosophy. We think the Jews and immigrants are a threat to America and we're not afraid to state that publicly."

Leslie didn't want the atmosphere to get too heated so she quickly changed the focus of the discussion. "Are you men concerned that the sniper's choice of victims may include some of you?"

Midler stepped in here. "Of course we are. We don't want some deranged Jew taking shots at us. You may disagree with our ideology but that doesn't mean we don't have families we love, and jobs we carry out with serious intent. We're just people like you are. We have our personal histories too. The sniper doesn't care about any of that. Our shared ideology is all he cares about. He's a sick man."

Leslie complimented Midler on his thoughtful comment. "That's a good point, Mr. Midler. You made it very clear."

Gary moved the discussion along. "What are you doing about that? So far the police and FBI don't have any leads to go on. The killing may continue."

The room was silent again.

Gary continued, "The sniper seemed to be triggered at first by attacks on Jewish gatherings. Now he may have decided on a less restrictive agenda. He seems to believe that the attackers are only a small part of a larger army of neo-Nazi sympathizers and that all components of that army are fair game. He obviously hasn't been going after the actual perpetrators of those attacks." Gary sat down.

A third man stood up and identified himself. "I'm Henry Grey. I'm a bus driver for the city of New York. We're all friends here. We're a community. We have common beliefs. *We* haven't committed any crimes. The sniper is a murderer. We're puzzled by the inability of the FBI to find this killer and eliminate him. I'll say it if the others won't: we wonder if the Jewish influence over our government has extended to the FBI." He sat down.

Leslie pursued that point. "Do any of you share that concern with Henry Grey?"

All the men raised their hands.

Leslie continued on a different path. "Does the term 'neo-Nazi' apply to your views? It's a term widely employed in law enforcement and in most major newspapers? I wouldn't be surprised if the sniper has identified his victims as neo-Nazis."

Midler answered for the group, "It's not a term we use to describe ourselves, but it has been applied to us by others. It's a convenient shorthand and naturally contains many implications that are faulty. For instance, none of us in this room advocate the genocide of Jews."

Gary stood up again to claim the floor. "Let me ask this, do you have a plan to counter the threat posed by the sniper?"

The room was quiet.

"I guess the answer is no."

Vogel rose and said his paper was encouraging readers to keep their eyes and ears open and report any suspicious activity to the authorities. He also added that they were encouraged to report any such activities to his paper since the police and FBI seemed to be impotent in the face of the "killer Jew."

Leslie and Gary nodded to each other, agreeing that the meeting was over.

"Thank you, gentlemen. We appreciate hearing your views on this pressing matter. Here are our business cards. If any of you think of any ideas that we didn't hit on that need to be expressed, please give either of us a call."

Midler led them to the door and thanked them for listening to the men. He hoped the newspaper might do something about what seemed to be a dangerous situation for them all.

Driving away, Leslie opined that the men felt helpless and espoused the standard anti-Semitic party line. She told Gary that the sniper would have been pleased if he'd been a fly on the wall.

CHAPTER TWENTY-SIX

G rey, cold, and rainy. Bert Alder thought it was only appropriate he bury his mother on such a day. Her entire life had been lived under dark clouds. She'd persevered and devoted her life to her son. Once he was out of the house and on his own she had no one to share her gloom with on a daily basis. He visited often and on most of his visits she recalled the horror the Nazi SS visited on her family in Stroudheim. She rarely reminisced about her childhood when her beautiful family was intact and happy, even as the dark curtain of Nazism in Germany was beginning to descend over them. When he was with her, Bert did all he could to keep her depression from overwhelming her. He succeeded to a degree but it was for naught. She'd slide right back into it as soon as the door closed behind him.

Now she was gone. A pain-free ending came during her sleep. *Thank God,* he thought. *A peaceful ending.*

Terry had been an exceptional daughter-in-law. She continued to look in on Sophie after she and Bert were divorced. Now she and Bert spoke as they walked under umbrellas, away from the gravesite.

Bert spoke in a somber tone, "I couldn't have wished her a more peaceful way out. She at least deserved that as a final act."

"Bert, you were a wonderful son. You did all you could, considering her despair."

"You know, Terry, I wonder if the sniper gave her a measure of satisfaction. We talked very little about it. I'd like to believe she understood what he was doing. It raised a rare smile on her lips. There was hate deep inside her that couldn't be reconciled."

They were nearly at their cars.

"Terry, maybe the sniper was the son she really needed. He was the only source of vengeance for her. It would never be enough but it was a payback for all that had been taken away from her."

She stared at Bert with a quizzical smile. "I never heard you so passionate on any subject. Whatever effect it had is moot now, Bert. Sophie is gone and she'll never tell us what, if any, effect the sniper killings had on her."

Bert stood still a moment and seemed to be in a deeply reflective mood.

"Terry, I have to believe that she would have encouraged the sniper killings. That she considered them justified. She would have considered them a memorial for her lost family. After all these years of brooding, something was happening that she could take pleasure in."

Terry said nothing. She was surprised at Bert's persistence in lauding the sniper killings. The Bert she'd known was never this philosophical. She attributed this to Sophie's death and the end of a very close mother-son relationship.

"Bert, let's go have lunch and try to revive some happy memories of Sophie. I know she didn't have many, but that makes the few we can recall that much more meaningful. Let's try the deli on Columbus and 89th Street. I'll meet you there."

Driving back to Manhattan from the cemetery in Queens, Terry was fixated on something Bert had said: Maybe the sniper was the son she really needed. It was as if he wished *he* was the sniper. What a crazy notion! Bert, a sniper, killing five or six innocent men? That didn't sound at all like him. At least not until their conversation in the cemetery.

Against her better judgment she was going to check the nights of the killings against her work schedule. Did she work late on all those dates? Maybe there was no concordance. That would serve as an alibi and cancel out this nutty idea.

Over the ensuing few days, Bert began to feel as if a weight had been lifted off his shoulders. It engendered guilt in him to think of his mother as a burden. He now saw that the death of Sophie allowed him to see Terry in a new light, one free of Sophie's unspoken competition for his love. It also brought to the fore the conflicted anger he felt unconsciously toward Sophie for her domination of him all through his childhood. His emotions were in turmoil.

The sniper would continue out of deep respect for his mother and her horrific loss, but his underlying motivation was being reexamined in the light of her death.

CHAPTER TWENTY-SEVEN

On the pretext of meeting for a drink before going out to dinner, Leslie found herself in Gary's apartment. He mixed two vodka martinis and handed her one.

She sat back on the sofa and complimented him on his bartending skill. He approached her, set down his drink, bent down, and kissed her fully on the lips. She responded by returning the kiss with a hand behind his head, pulling his face and lips harder into hers. The mood was unmistakable. Gary sat down alongside Leslie. They put their arms around each other and resumed intense kissing. Without any words clothing was shed. It was as if they'd agreed on a plan and had no need talk about it.

She lay back on the sofa and he entered her. They were so ready it was impossible to prolong the intense feeling. One moment they were on the summit and a minute or two later they were basking in the after-effect of a powerful orgasm.

"I knew it would be special, Gary. We needed to complete our picture. I feel so close to you."

"We knew this was coming, Leslie, and we both wanted it badly."

Leslie added emphatically, "And how."

CHAPTER TWENTY-EIGHT

A bright and sunny morning was perfect for walking to the Hebrew Day School. Len Cramer and his girls, ages six and nine, were two blocks from the school when they stopped at the bakery for their favorite snacks, chocolate chip cookies. As they left the bakery they heard several loud explosions coming from the direction of the school, followed by screaming and more explosions. As they were about to round the last street corner before the school entrance, people were running toward them, screaming. Len drew back and pulled his girls close to him. No more explosions were heard but sirens were approaching from several directions.

Len cautiously peered around the corner. Bodies of adults and children were scattered near the school entrance. People were either standing around, bewildered, or attempting to help the fallen victims of some kind of attack. Len held his girls back, not letting them see the carnage. Ambulances and police cars arrived and began tending to the injured.

The Utica Post reported the next day that two gunmen had gotten out of a car near the school entrance, shot and killed the guard on duty, and then shot people indiscriminately, killing three adults and seven children. Four others were wounded. The gunmen then fled in their car before any call for help could be made. Before driving away they scattered leaflets extolling Nazi virtues.

There was no question that this was a hate crime. The FBI raised the suspicion that the same two gunmen may have been responsible for the synagogue shooting in Albany several months before. There was some ballistic evidence suggesting this, but no hard evidence. The eyewitnesses in the Utica shooting could only offer general descriptions of the gunmen. They were white, male, and appeared young. There was little or nothing else to go on.

Bert Alder watched the evening news coverage alone in his apartment. He saw this event as a direct challenge to the sniper. The neo-Nazis wanted to demonstrate that they were undeterred, showing the futility of his killings in the New York area.

Perhaps it didn't have any relevance to the sniper shootings.

Assuming the killers in Albany and Utica were one and the same, some sniper work in their backyard would be helpful to raise their awareness of the danger attached to their vicious killings. He'd have to create a list of targets in the area between Albany and Utica, New York. Then he'd have to find a way to act on it without leaving any tracks for the authorities to follow. This presented a considerable challenge. On reflection he saw too many pitfalls and decided it was a bad idea.

CHAPTER TWENTY-NINE

Gary and Leslie were sitting in her kitchen planning their next step in the sniper saga. They were sure the school killings were going to awaken the sniper, who had been lying low since the Staten Island shootings.

The six-pack of Stellas had only two bottles left. A bowl of chips on the table was nearly empty.

"Gary, we have enough for a good story based on our visit with Midler and his friends. Throw in your visit with the Jewish leaders and it's a good piece. Trouble is it doesn't bring us any closer to solving the sniper riddle. It's a different story if we have some fresh information about the sniper."

They stared at their warming bottles of beer. Leslie brought out the idea of an open letter that Howard had suggested.

"What about an open letter to the sniper? We ask him to explain himself. If he takes us up on our invitation he may give away some useful information that the FBI has been unable to discover. He may be tempted to reply to us. He's obviously harboring a hatred for the Nazis and probably has no one to share his ideas with. At least I think he has no one. Might be worth a shot."

"That's a great idea, Les. The tone of the letter can't be too sympathetic, but it can't be hostile and accusatory. We could get some guidance from a psychiatrist. One who knows human behavior better than we do."

"I like it, Gary. Let's do it. We each search for a shrink with the background we're after. Then we put our heads together and pick one.

"First let's check with our editor before we make any move in this direction. We'll need Livingstone firmly in our corner before we use the paper as a vehicle to communicate with a serial killer."

CHAPTER THIRTY

George Harris was the author of two books dealing with the psychology of hate crimes and a professor of psychology at Fordham University. Leslie and Gary agreed he was the right man to offer them advice before they wrote their open letter. They hurriedly scanned his books before meeting with him in his office at Fordham.

The university had a very somber look, with many older grey stone buildings. Harris's office was housed in one of them, identified by a single-word sign on the lawn: Psychology.

Harris was expecting the visitors and greeted them warmly as they stood in the doorway to his office. He was dressed casually in corduroy slacks, an open collar dress shirt, and a grey cardigan sweater. He resembled the picture on his books' inside back cover. A tall, grey-haired man, clean-shaven, with somewhat uneven teeth that drew attention when he smiled.

After introductions and some friendly chatter, Professor Harris began the discussion. He restated their objective.

"You want to print an open letter to the sniper, a man you've never met, asking that he state his justification for killing men he believes to be neo-Nazis? He's a blank slate to you with the one exception being his record of killings. You're asking me to help you put together a 'letter' that will inform your readers and, if he responds, possibly lure him into revealing something about himself that brings you closer to identifying him."

Leslie responded, "That's it, Professor. Here's what we think we know about the sniper. He's very clever. He's evaded detection by being careful. He picks his targets with care. He's in no hurry to carry out his killings. He targets men he identifies as neo-Nazis and harbors a deeply felt hatred. We know nothing of a personal nature about him except that he's likely Jewish, though not necessarily. Oh yes, he's a very good marksman with a sniper rifle. That's it."

Gary affirmed that he and Leslie were on the same page. "Good summation, Leslie. Your turn, Professor."

"Okay. I agree with what you two have surmised. This man—and I believe it could be a man or a woman—is not a classic serial killer. He has chosen his targets with care and believes he's doing something justifiable in the eyes of reasonable men. There *is* a justification here and it's not very far out. In fact, the Jewish community may have many members who are ambivalent about his action. It turns on the term 'justifiable.'"

Leslie recalled Howard's similar analysis. He and Gary each described the sniper as mature, intelligent, and not an unhinged killer.

Professor Harris continued, "Society won't condone his action, but society doesn't interpret circumstances as he does. Allowing people to interpret conditions in a manner that allows citizens to kill whoever they identify as transgressors takes us over a line we dare not cross as a society. Other societies, in the name of religion or tradition, may cross that line. For example, stoning an unmarried daughter who becomes sexually involved with a married man. We will not allow that type of killing in America.

"What is this man's trigger point? Why now? Assuming we know what his goal is, killing neo-Nazis to stop their crimes against Jews, why does he break out now? This is where the psychology kicks in. Something personal has pushed him in a direction that he otherwise was long able to resist. Maybe he was teetering on the brink for a long time and it didn't take much to tip him over. The synagogue massacre was an immediate trigger but it wasn't the first anti-Semitic attack.

"Perhaps some recent life-event set him off. He became the sniper to offset that setback. Remember, we're looking for something in his personal life that made sniping a way to restore his self-esteem. He may have been beset by more than one sorrow in his life. At least that's a theory. In your letter to him I'd advise a sympathetic tone. He's suffering and has found an outlet to relieve his sadness. That outlet is not totally outlandish. Our society won't condone it but that's because of the extreme measure he's applying. His vengeance is not so far afield."

Harris paused and Leslie took this as a moment to step in.

"Thank you, Doctor. I think you've given us some direction. We'll put together a piece for our paper and ask for your comments before we file it."

The reporters left and walked to their car deep in thought.

"Gary, he was helpful, but I still feel we're too far from the sniper to understand what drives him. The letter will be more of a challenge for us than for him."

CHAPTER THIRTY-ONE

The Salad Bar was a popular lunch spot in midtown Manhattan. It was one of many. Women on perpetual diets could always find some low-cal fare to stay within their caloric constraints. Terry Alder and Diane Bowman were two such lunch customers. With big bowls of leaves before them they brought each other up to date on their lives.

Jammed in with the hungry lunch crowd at two prized counter seats, Diane had no hesitation probing her friend's private life, "Terry, you've been single now for nearly two months. Has the dust settled on that chapter of your life?"

"Sort of. Sometimes I miss Bert, but those moments are fewer and farther between as time passes. I have no regret about our parting. I know you're a long time veteran of the marriage wars. Your divorce from Gabe was over two years ago. Ancient history. Are you dating anyone now?"

The conversation continued in the personal vein for half an hour. Their salad bowls were empty and the waiting customers were eyeing their two seats.

"We ought to move on, Diane. Those hungry vultures on the line can see our bowls are about empty. We can talk outside." They left the restaurant.

Out on the street with people racing by in both directions, Diane could sense Terry had something more to say.

"Out with it, Terry. You're itching to tell me something."

"Okay, Di, hear me out. Bert's mother passed away recently. You know how close they were. You met Sophie. A lovely woman nearing ninety. Well, I went to the funeral in Queens. Sophie and I were close. As close as you can be with an elderly mother-in-law. In any event, Bert and I had a private moment as we walked to our cars.

"I know he was under considerable stress, having just buried his mother. He brought up the sniper matter. He was obsessed with it. He saw the sniper as Sophie's ideal son. The sniper killings were justified as vengeance for Sophie, a memorial for her. He saw the sniper's killings only as they related to Sophie. It was odd. I'd never seen Bert so passionate about anything, I'd never seen Bert passionate, period. I got this crazy idea. Could Bert be the sniper? I know it sounds crazy, but you weren't there at the funeral."

"Terry, I can't picture Bert Alder as a sniper knocking off guys around the city."

"I know, I know. It sounds crazy. Well, I know in our last days of marriage we were apart many nights, eating dinner alone in restaurants after work. I did some research. I checked the nights all the sniper killings occurred while we were still living together and matched them with my late work nights. I was looking for a mismatch that would serve as an alibi for Bert, an evening we were both together and a sniper killing took place. I think you can guess. There weren't any. There were five sniper shootings and I was very late at work on every one of them. When I work late I get home around eleven. He knows that. That's all I have, Diane. I don't know what to do. For the moment I'm letting it rest. I just had to tell someone and you drew the short straw."

"Wow. There's no evidence of anything, Terry. It's all just far out speculation. I can't tell you what to do. A lot of people are sympathetic with the sniper even though they believe his killings are wrong. I don't know if you saw *The Times* this morning. It carries an open letter to the sniper. Read it and think about the matter some more. Maybe you should talk to the reporters who wrote the letter. I don't know, I just can't see Bert in that role. Gotta run! Read the paper. Love you."

CHAPTER THIRTY-TWO

"Here's the letter I drafted, Gary. I think it contains all the issues we wanted to put out there. I ran it by the police and they had no objection to its content."

An open letter to the sniper

> *This letter is our effort to learn all we can about your motivation and goals regarding the shooting campaign. You've probably read the several pieces we've authored in this paper. We've tried to be objective in our reporting. At the outset, though, we must state that we don't condone murder. This letter is an effort to have you express your thoughts regarding the shootings. If there are mitigating circumstances, and we suspect there are, we and the public would like to hear them.*

There is a great deal of conjecture surrounding the shootings. Some of it is more sympathetic than you may imagine. This is your opportunity to explain your position to the public.

We cannot guarantee that our paper will publish your response, in toto or in part, before we've had an opportunity to read it.

Should you choose to respond to this letter, send your response to the address below:

Leslie Nugent and Gary Hoffman
The New York Times Company
620 Eighth Avenue
New York, NY 10018

"It reads well, Leslie. It's an open invitation to someone we don't know. All we can do now is hope he reads *The Times* and check our mail for a response. Good show, Les."

CHAPTER THIRTY-THREE

Terry Alder called Bert and set up a time for them to get together. They agreed to meet at her apartment (formerly their apartment) the following night after work. Terry planned to confront him on the subject of his identity as the sniper. She had no idea how he was going to react. She had no evidence to go on. Her main concern was for Bert and his state of mind. She hoped he could dissuade her from the nagging notion she was carrying with her.

She was also curious to know what he made of the open letter in *The Times*. Of course, that depended on how he identified with the sniper. As she lived with her notion it became more and more plausible, even if Diane found it too improbable to accept.

Her workday drew to a close. The sun was gone and the streetlights were on. It was after seven and Terry found herself on a bus going home to her apartment. She tried out different approaches in her mind, none of which buoyed her confidence. She wished she didn't feel so alone. Having Diane along would have helped.

Bert coming over to the apartment they'd lived in together gave her an uneasy feeling. She couldn't explain it. Her life hadn't gotten back on track after the divorce and she felt adrift.

Bert rang the doorbell and she let him in. He greeted Terry with a big smile and a friendly kiss on her cheek. She was still uncertain how she was going to approach him. He seemed relaxed and this had the effect of calming her nerves a bit. Bert was dressed in what looked like the clothes he came home from work in.

"Make yourself comfortable, Bert. I'm gonna have some wine. Would you join me?"

"Sure, sounds good. I'll have what you're having."

She went into the kitchen and came back with two cold glasses of Chablis. They went into the living room and sat at opposite ends of a sofa

"I didn't plan dinner, Bert. I didn't know whether you had any plans for the evening. We could always call in for take-out."

They became uncomfortably quiet. Terry knew she had to break the ice. "Well, Bert, I'm gonna dive right in. I'm a little nervous so bear with me." She paused a moment and then began to speak slowly.

"It started when we were walking back from Sophie's gravesite. You were talking about the sniper and how his activity impinged on Sophie. I know you were distraught but I'd never heard you so passionate about any subject. It was disconcerting. I hardly knew you. Since then I've been mulling over what you said. "I know it's a far reach but I began to picture *you* as the sniper. It seems so out of character, but when seen in the context of your devotion to Sophie it began to seem less implausible."

Bert was staring intensely at her. He said not a word.

"I was looking for an alibi for you so I could rid myself of this obsession. I checked the five nights of the shootings on my calendar. I worked late every one of them. I was hoping that we were together on at least one. That would have provided the alibi I wanted for you. So there you have it, Bert. No hard evidence of anything. Just a nagging concern of mine. Bert, are you the sniper?"

Bert smiled at his former wife and shook his head from side to side.

"Terry, I don't recall what I said after the gravesite ceremony. You said I was distraught. That's putting it mildly. You know how much Sophie meant to me. My admiration for the sniper and how his work seemed to play so well in Sophie's final days is an accurate reflection on how I feel even today. I don't think I'm the only Jew who feels this way about these vengeful acts. Secondly, during the last days of our marriage we often worked late, probably to avoid uncomfortable nights at home together. I'm sure you could document many nights when you weren't home and couldn't provide an alibi for me when the sniper was *not* active. No, Terry. I'm not the sniper. Sometimes I wish I was."

Terry wasn't sure how to proceed. There it was: outright denial. Now what? Just drop the matter? She wasn't sure if she was ready to do that. She was hoping for some exculpatory evidence. Her legal training had kicked in and was making it hard for her to walk away from her original premise.

"I guess I'll have to let it rest, Bert."

"You don't sound convinced, Terry. What more can I do?"

"You've done all you can, Bert. Let's just drop the matter."

"Consider it dropped. Now, can I buy you dinner? There's that good Lebanese place only one short block from here."

"Sure, Bert. Lead the way."

Putting on her coat, Terry mused that this didn't seem like the Bert Alder she'd only recently divorced. This was a friendlier, more welcoming guy. She'd always been attracted to him physically, but this was a warmer Bert than she'd known. She liked this version and saw herself even lapsing into a mildly flirtatious mode. Their history together made it easy for her to envision them together, and not just over dinner.

CHAPTER THIRTY-FOUR

There were several responses to *the Times* letter in her mailbox. Two were clearly written by nut jobs. The other four were serious letters, but each one could be discounted as not having the feeling of authenticity. Gary's mailbox had a similar collection of letters. It was a disappointing start.

Leslie's landline phone rang and call-waiting showed no name for the caller.

She suspected it was coming from a throw-away phone. Desperate for any serious response, she took the call.

"This is Leslie. What can I do for you?"

"I'd like to respond to the letter. Will you give me the time?"

Leslie heard a man's voice and detected no anxiety in his manner of speech.

"I've got all day if you've got anything that rings true." She turned on the recorder in case this was the real thing.

"I'm going to record this conversation. I just wanted you to know."

"I have no problem with that. Just hear me out. I know that many people consider me a murderer, pure and simple. Well, what I've been doing *is* rather simple but I don't think it should be dismissed as the act of a person with no conscience. To the contrary; the shootings *are* acts of conscience. I consider the neo-Nazis to have declared war on the Jewish people. My role in the war is to respond in-kind to their reckless killing of innocent people. In war both sides pay a price; until I began shooting, their side had paid no price. All the killings were on the Jewish side. And I emphasize, *all* the killings. Now the pain is being shared. Can you understand this? If you accept my premise that there is a war going on, you'll be sympathetic to what I'm trying to accomplish. I'm only one person so I can inflict only a few casualties on the other side."

He paused. "Do you want to ask me anything? Just don't try to identify me."

Leslie was stunned. This caller had the ring of authenticity. She'd signaled for Gary to listen in and he caught most of the conversation. She wrote him a one word note: "authentic?" He nodded his head in the affirmative.

"Sir, I've listened very closely. I do have a few questions. There have been no shootings since the Staten Island killings. Do you intend to keep going? Is this just a temporary lull?"

"It depends on what the other side does. If there are continued atrocities, I will respond. If they shut down their killers, I will stand down. I have no timetable so I can't respond to your question with any certainty. Anything else?"

Gary handed her a piece of paper with a question.

"Is there any way we can keep this dialogue going? Perhaps schedule another telephone call after we've digested what you had to say?"

"I'll call you again next week so we can continue this conversation. Just don't try to 'unmask' me. If you do, I'll have to end our connection."

The line went dead. Leslie leaned back in her chair. Perspiration stained her shirt. Gary couldn't stop his head from turning back and forth.

"Articulate, male, and composed. No frothing-at-the-mouth, rabid, madman," was Gary's take on the caller. "He clearly spelled out his justification."

"We can write this up as the sniper's response to our letter, but we have no way of proving he's the sniper, Gary. Next time we have to ask him some questions that will prove he's the guy. We need to ask for some information we haven't printed that's only known to the police and the shooter. Maybe Lionel Cobb can help us with this."

That evening, in a quiet restaurant mostly empty late on a weekday night, Leslie shared her transcript with Howard Marcus. She and Howard had been out of touch for over a week so he welcomed her invitation to meet. He'd been reluctant to pursue her after several of his calls had gone unanswered. He was puzzled by her distance, but was willing to help her with the sniper story.

Howard offered some initial thoughts. "Cool, and totally under control. Not a hint of what's driving him. He's not going to be tricked into giving away any information about himself. I'm convinced there's a deep flaw in his personal life that he keeps under lock and key. Revenge is the obvious motive but it has to be personal to drive him to this extreme. And there has to be some recent life event or events that pushed him to take an active role *at this time*. The latter could be generic, not directly connected to the vengeance he's now pursuing."

"Howard, we have the shootings, the telephone conversation, and your take on the sniper's motivation. Trouble is it still leaves us far from any deeper understanding of the man. Too many pieces are missing from this puzzle, Howard. How are we going to penetrate into his real psyche? One thing I took away from that phone call was his willingness, even eagerness, to explain himself. I think he's so obsessed with remaining secret that he's lonely. Most people want to share their special experience with another person. He's missing that. Now here's the big question: How can I become that person?"

"That's a good thought, Leslie. Get close to him without knowing *who* he is and he might be willing to open up somewhat. I like that. I might normally worry about your safety but in this case I don't. This man is not a killer in that sense. He's not homicidal except in that one situation that's driving him."

"I'm going to give this some serious thought, Howard. Hopefully he'll call again and give me an opportunity to try out a strategy. Right now it's just a goal without a pathway. I'm going to change the subject and tell you my most immediate step is a meeting with Lionel Cobb to identify some facts about the shootings that will allow us to authenticate the caller as the sniper. That's an imperative."

Howard had more to say and it wasn't about the sniper. "Leslie, we both know there's been a noticeable cooling in our relationship. I don't understand what's caused that. We were cruising along on a very promising path. Now we're back to just 'good friends.' Help me out here."

"This is difficult for me, Howard. I started seeing another guy about the time I met you. His and my relationship took off. I knew you were seriously looking at big jobs out west. I didn't want to deal with that eventuality. I'm sorry. Really sorry. I think we were a good pairing. It was a difficult decision for me and I certainly didn't want to hurt you."

"I'm okay, Leslie. I knew we had cooled off. And you're right about that job hunt. I've been offered the department chairmanship at the University of Oregon and they have my tentative acceptance. I'm glad you leveled with me. I knew your concern about long distance courtships and I'd been hesitating about telling you."

"I'm happy for you, Howard, and I'm glad we cleared the air about us."

CHAPTER THIRTY-FIVE

Alone in his apartment, many thoughts were running through his mind. Bert reflected on the phone call. He was sure he didn't give away any information that would lead the police to him. That was essential. He felt good about getting out his message. Up until now that message resided in his mind alone and that bothered him. Now he'd let the newspaper amplify what he intended the neo-Nazis to recognize as the harsh reality. He was anxious to see how the press dealt with the phone call.

On the more mundane side, he reflected on his meeting with Terry. He sensed a change in her attitude toward him. He wasn't sure if he convinced her that he wasn't the sniper. She seemed to come away uncertain about that. At least he had softened her suspicion.

He also could feel a renewed attraction on her part as well as his. Something had changed for each of them. She must have felt he was a different man than the one she'd lived with for the past years. He felt it too.

Having a commitment to something big had made him more resolute. That was reflected in his general behavior and she found that appealing. He had never seen his feelings for her diminish the way her feelings for him had. The force drawing them back to each other was worth pursuing.

Three days after his phone call to the reporter there was still no recognition that a call had even taken place. He'd give it a few more days before calling again.

CHAPTER THIRTY-SIX

When Lionel Cobb was told about the phone call he nearly fell off his chair. This could end the logjam holding up the investigation. Leslie explained her strategy to authenticate the caller. She was asking Cobb to think of a few details about the shootings that were not public knowledge. If the caller could amplify on them it could confirm his identity as the sniper. He immediately went to his notes on each shooting and culled out the kind of information Leslie was after.

There wasn't a lot of information held back from the press. Ballistic information was not of great interest to the press so much of that detail never made it into print. The police knew the type of ammunition used. It was the same at every shooting, but it couldn't tell them the name of the weapon used. If they had the weapon they could match it to the bullets used. That was it. Leslie could ask the sniper what type of ammunition he was using. If he had the right answer that would be a measure of authenticity. There was nothing else he could offer Leslie.

Leslie was grateful for the ballistic information. It was something. She'd try it out on the sniper if she heard from him again. The lack of authentication was holding back her story about the phone call and the sniper's philosophy.

The murder of two yeshiva students driving on a relatively isolated road in Rockland County, New York was a major story on the evening news. A young girl, twelve years old, riding in the back of the car had hidden on the floor and was able to make several important observations: the killers were two in number and male, they rode motorcycles, they wore leather jackets with "A for A" stenciled in big white letters on the back of their jackets. The picture was clear. The cyclists must have tailed the car when it left the yeshiva. They forced the car off the road as it passed through a wooded area. They then shot the two students as they sat in their car. The young girl hidden in the back was lucky to be alive. "A for A" undoubtedly stood for "America for Americans." An open and shut hate crime.

The Rockland County Police stopped and questioned all the motorcyclists in their territory. The girl, unfortunately, was unable to identify the killers. She'd been hiding when they approached the car and knew enough to stay silent and out of sight. Only after the shooting did she get a look at the backs of the killers as they left the scene. The police were pessimistic about making an arrest.

Bert read the story and knew he'd have to respond. He slipped into his "sniper mode" and this distracted him from his thoughts about Terry. He had a list of potential targets and now set out to take one down. The proximity in time of a sniper killing and the murders in Rockland County would be unmistakable evidence of a revenge killing.

CHAPTER THIRTY-SEVEN

Henry Grey was a long-time veteran bus driver. He also was an outspoken member of America for Americans and a frequent contributor to neo-Nazi newspapers and magazines.

Bert called the bus company headquarters to find out Henry Grey's work hours and route. He said he was a close friend and had personal information about a sick relative to give him when he came off shift. The person in the dispatcher's office was quite cooperative. She told him Grey drove a Number 53 bus and was expected to pull into the bus garage at roughly 8:05 p.m. She said he'd been driving for nearly twenty years and was a stickler for keeping on schedule.

Bert sat in a shadowed parking spot near the bus garage. The garage was a very large, depressing one-story structure filled with blue and white city buses. There were no people just hanging around. Drivers delivered their buses and were quick to leave the area. There was nothing to hang around for.

THE SNIPER

Bert was parked up the street from the yawning entrance to the garage. He had seen several buses go in and seen men dressed in grey pants and shirt, some with waist length jackets, presumably drivers, emerge minutes later and head to their cars in the nearby parking lot. He had a good view of the entrance and the parking area. The street leading into the garage was lined with trees on both sides.

Shortly after eight, a blue and white Number 53 bus pulled into the garage. Bert had his rifle in his lap. No other buses had entered the garage in the last ten minutes or so. He assumed the next man to exit the garage would be Henry Grey. A man emerged and headed to the parking lot. Through his telescopic rifle site Bert could see a rather young man. He hesitated. Having no picture of his target he relied on his instinct.

This felt wrong. He put the gun back in his lap. The young man got in his car and left the parking lot. Not two minutes later another blue and white Number 53 bus pulled into the garage. *Of course*, he thought, more than one bus drove Route 53. A slight sweat broke out on his back. He'd nearly killed an innocent man. How stupid of him not to have good identification stats or a picture.

The man who emerged next was an older white male. The woman in the office said he'd been driving for nearly twenty years. This man had to be Henry Grey. Bert put the crosshairs on his target's head and fired a single shot. The red explosion told him he'd hit his target and that his night's work was done. He slowly pulled out of his parking spot, turned around and drove home.

CHAPTER THIRTY-EIGHT

Early morning found Leslie in a mostly empty newsroom. Her desk phone rang. 'Call waiting' said Herman Midler was on the phone for Leslie. She couldn't think of any reason why he'd be calling her. They had no business pending.

"Hello, Mr. Midler. What can I do for you?"

"I'm trying to control myself, Ms. Nugent. Henry Grey was murdered tonight and the police think it was the sniper. I want to know if you're in any way responsible for his death. Did you print his name in your newspaper and set him up as a target? Your answer better be no."

"My answer is an unequivocal no! I haven't put the names of any of the people I met in your house in any article I've written. I think the sniper has his own method for identifying targets and so far he's been consistent. His victims have all been outspoken believers in the issues we discussed with you. I'm sorry about Henry Grey's death. We all want this killing to end, but the violence inciting it also has to end. The murders upstate of the two students only serve to spur on the sniper."

"Henry Grey had no hand in that."

"We discussed that Mr. Midler. The sniper doesn't care who's guilty or who's innocent in each specific tragedy. As far as he's concerned all people who espouse the Nazi philosophy are members of the same army and are fair game for him to return fire. That's all I have to say."

"I hope your hands are clean, Ms. Nugent, and you can sleep peacefully at night."

He hung up. Leslie was shaken, not from the call, but rather from the news of another killing. Since the upstate killing she'd been expecting a sniper response.

Less than an hour later, her phone rang again and the number was not one she recognized. The voice was familiar. The male caller spoke in an even tone.

"Yes, it's me, Ms. Nugent. I was calling to find out why my response to your open letter hadn't made it into print."

"I'm glad you finally called. I couldn't print your response because I couldn't authenticate your identity as the sniper. Let's try to do that now. The killing last night hasn't made it into print so your knowledge of the event could help with that. Are you willing to go on?"

"Here's all you need to know, Ms. Nugent. The victim was Henry Grey and he was killed with one head shot as he came out of the Metropolitan bus garage in the Kingsbridge section of the Bronx. He was a known neo-Nazi spokesperson. Is that good enough?"

"I don't have the police report on hand, so I hope you'll give me a few hours to see how your information stacks up against that. One bit of evidence I do have is the type of ammunition you use. Can you tell me that?"

"No problem. I use 7.62A-51mm NATO 'short-action' cartridges. Does that match up with your information?"

"It does. I'll follow up on the other information you gave me and if it also checks out there'll be a piece in the paper covering the conversation we had a week ago."

"That's all I needed to know."

"One more thing. It would be helpful if I had some way to reach you."

"Not necessary. I'll stay in touch. Good-bye." He disconnected.

Leslie was immediately on the phone to Gary.

CHAPTER THIRTY-NINE

Late night meetings were not unusual in the news department. The department ran 24/7 and took on urgent stories as a matter of course, whenever they took place. John Livingstone, the editor overseeing Leslie and Gary, had agreed to review the sniper story in light of the authentication phone call.

"I agree with you both. The guy's for real. I also agree that we need to print some version of his initial response to your 'open letter.' What are you two thinking?"

Leslie let Gary have the floor. She felt a bit guilty being the one who fielded both calls from the sniper, especially when Gary wasn't around for the second one.

"We've agreed that a near verbatim version should go out. I think this will help establish our credibility with him, and also because the response should be *his* and not some doctored version of ours."

"You said 'near verbatim,' Gary? How *near* will it be?" asked the editor.

"Okay. Let's make it verbatim," was Leslie's first contribution.

"I agree. Let me see what you put together before we send it out. I'm damned curious to see what kind of mail we receive once the public reads it."

"I called Lionel Cobb so he's up to date on this communication. Neither of us saw this bringing us any closer to identifying the sniper. It does give us a better picture of what's driving him. That may prove useful at some later time. Cobb is surprised we haven't seen any copycat shooters. He thinks some like-minded individual or individuals will be inspired to take similar action, independent of the original sniper. That person would not just be an imitator but someone with personal motivation. He worried it could get out of hand."

CHAPTER FORTY

The sniper story in *The Times* caused sales to soar. "Sold Out" was a term rarely heard at the paper. Leslie's and Gary's phones had to be transferred to a dedicated bank of answering operators. There was no way the two reporters could handle the call volume. On the other hand they wanted to get a sense of the public's sentiment, so they took as many calls as they personally could handle. Although sentiment ranged all the way from hate directed at Jews to deep sympathy for the sniper, the calls generally showed empathy for the sniper. The answering operators confirmed the two reporters' reading of the tenor of the calls.

This came as no surprise to Gary or Leslie. They felt that the sniper's initial call had been temperate. People understood his position even if they abhorred the murders. Each neo-Nazi atrocity had gradually moved public opinion toward a more positive feeling about the sniper. "Acceptance" was uncommon but "empathy" was heard in many calls. More than one caller likened the sniper to actor Charles Bronson as Paul

Kersey in the 1974 film *Death Wish*. In that film an architect seeks vengeance against street criminals who murdered his wife and left his daughter brain damaged. He becomes a vigilante killer of street criminals and evolves into a popular folk hero.

Howard and Leslie met for dinner at his invitation. He told her that he'd finally accepted the appointment at Oregon and would be leaving in two weeks. This was a farewell dinner. Leslie toasted to his certain success and his start of a new life far from New York City.

Howard took this opportunity to discuss the sniper for one last time.

"Leslie, I'm a secular Jew. Many in my more religious family are supportive of the sniper. They understand his position and wonder why more sympathizers haven't taken up arms. The 'Never Again' cry is being heard among sniper sympathizers. My liberal friends in the Jewish community prefer to leave it to law enforcement to resolve the matter. As usual, the Jewish community is fractured."

Howard wound down his discussion with some final thoughts. "The public's reactions are understandable but the sniper stands alone. He's not trying to establish a movement and lead it. This is one man's personal crusade. His reasoned approach to neo-Nazi killings is easy to understand but his response is far out. What accounts for this one man taking such a radical approach? It has to be personal."

That was what intrigued him, he told her.

He and Leslie parted good friends.

CHAPTER FORTY-ONE

Midler chose the airport at Nashville as a convenient place to meet people from all over the country. He felt Chicago O'Hare was even more convenient for travelers from the two coasts, but it was very carefully monitored. Meeting in Nashville was less conspicuous.

Erich Voigt checked in at the appointed airport hotel and relaxed in his room with a J&B scotch from the minibar. His flight from Boise got him into Nashville with several hours to spare before the meeting. Midler had called the meeting for 9:00 p.m. That gave all eight attendees plenty of time to get in and get settled in their rooms. The meeting would include dinner, so that left more time to relax.

Voigt knew most of the other men from previous meetings. Lying on the bed, he reviewed articles on the sniper shootings that he'd saved from magazines and newspapers. Like most people he was puzzled by the failure of the police and FBI to capture or kill the sniper. That was the basis for the meeting: what *their* organization could do to rid themselves of a single Jew murderer. Hitler had exterminated millions and all they had to do was kill one. Letting the Jew kill them one at a time, over and over, made them seem impotent. The rank and file was restless, and for good reason. Well, maybe a plan will emerge from the meeting.

Midler called the meeting to order promptly at nine. He had asked for the meeting so it seemed natural for him to run it. America for Americans had no recognized leader. It was a loose affiliation of numerous local groups that adhered to the Nazi code of beliefs.

After a brief overview of the sniper story, Midler opened the floor for comments. He cautioned the men not to offer any rants about the sniper because they were all on the same page about him. What they needed was a plan of action to solve the sniper dilemma.

Richard Andrews from Austin offered up a plan that his local chapter had backed enthusiastically.

"We advocate hiring a skilled assassin to find the sniper and eliminate him."

A murmur of agreement ran through the group. Several indicated that their chapters would back such a plan. This seemed to be the direction the majority wanted the group to head in. Another plan was to double or triple the reward money offered by the FBI. The current reward was $100,000.

Midler indicated that the sniper confined his killings to the New York metropolitan area. A large network of volunteer 'watchers' could be put in place to identify a sniper suspect after any future violent action. Such a net would have many gaping holes in it, but could serve as an aid in capturing the shooter. Many in the group considered this approach too docile. They wanted a more aggressive plan.

A third plan called for a retaliatory sniper. Kill members of the Jewish leadership every time a member of the A for A organization was targeted. This was tit-for-tat. One trouble with this was that it could be traced back to the organization. The sniper they were after seemingly had no Jewish organization backing him and didn't need any. He was his own man. The idea of America for Americans going after a lone avenger wouldn't help their image. It would do the opposite.

After an hour of heated discussion, Midler decided to end the meeting.

"The group has apparently decided that obtaining the services of a skilled hunter/assassin is the best route to follow. The assassin will be free to choose his own method of catching and killing the sniper. A network of watchers would be his to use as he sees fit. Each group has pledged to raise $20,000 and go after other funds as well. Erich Voigt has volunteered to head the effort to identify a candidate for the job. He welcomes any recommendation from members."

The meeting ended on an optimistic note. The group retired to the hotel bar.

CHAPTER FORTY-TWO

The Bronx wholesale food market near Yankee Stadium was preparing to close. 10:00 p.m. was the official closing time. After a busy Friday shopping day, there was a lot of cleaning up to do. The cleanup crew was not daunted by the amount of food scraps on the concrete floor. Cleanup would be completed by midnight, leaving plenty of time for the food wholesalers to get in and restock the shelves. By 6:00 a.m. the place would be restored to the same condition it was in when the previous shopping day began.

Leonard's fish stand was already putting tomorrow's fish out on ice. Dolph Leonard, supervising his two workers, was satisfied that their workday was over. He dismissed the men and headed to the large parking lot carrying two bags of produce. Vendors enjoyed the luxury of parking spaces very close to the market entrance. He put the bags in the trunk of his car, got in, and drove out of the lot toward his home in Pelham Bay Park. He was unaware that he was being followed.

THE SNIPER

Leonard pulled into his driveway a little after 11:00 p.m. He got out of the car and took the bags out of the trunk. As he closed the trunk he was struck in the back by two bullets. He fell against the trunk, landing in the driveway and lay there. He was unobserved at this hour. It wasn't until thirty minutes later that his wife, waiting expectantly for his return, looked outside and saw his car. She came outside and found his body. He had bled to death from the two wounds.

Police cordoned off the driveway and waited for the forensics team to go over the body and search the area for any clues related to the shooting. The bullets that killed the victim were in his chest, so the autopsy would provide the homicide team with at least that bit of evidence. There was nothing else found in a wide perimeter around the victim. The area was densely populated with two family homes tightly packed together. There was no obvious place where a shooter could have hidden and had a good shot at the victim.

Leslie closely monitored police calls and caught this one just before she turned off her bedside lamp. The shooting could very well be another sniper kill. The victim's name wasn't one she recognized. A Google search didn't turn up anything on Dolph Leonard. That, she thought, would be unusual for the sniper. This would require some legwork on her part. Were there any persons who might have had a personal reason to kill the victim? Infidelity? Gambling debts? Shady business dealing? Last on the list was identification as a neo-Nazi supporter or organizer. She'd give this victim a thorough going-over before considering the case a possible sniper shooting.

CHAPTER FORTY-THREE

"I was expecting your call, Leslie. What took you so long? It's half past eight and I'm working on my third cup of coffee."

Leslie was pleased to be teased by the homicide detective. It was a sign he welcomed her into his world.

"What've you got, Lionel? I assume the family was questioned last night."

"There's not much to work with. Guy has a fish stall in the Bronx market and makes a modest living. He's married, seemingly happily, for twenty years. Has two kids in high school and carries a small mortgage on his house. Doesn't gamble. Has no big debts. Just an average working stiff now lying on a table in the morgue. The two bullets taken out of his chest are a bit bruised but are not identical to the ones we've been seeing in the sniper shootings. It's not likely the same gun was used in this shooting. That's about it, Leslie. Oh, one more thing. The wife says they both voted for Obama in 2008 and 2012. He's of Scandinavian descent and she, get this, is Jewish."

"The police on the case did a great job, Lionel. It doesn't look like this works for the sniper. Lord knows what it does work for. I'm going to give it some serious thought and get back to you later today, once I've solved the case."

She enjoyed teasing him, but did it infrequently enough so as not to jeopardize their special relationship.

"Thanks for sharing that database with me, Lionel."

Leslie was deep in thought at her desk when Gary happened by.

"Heard about the killing last night, Les. Police turn up anything of interest?"

"Sort of, Gary. It doesn't seem to work for the sniper. Or anyone else. Makes me think it was a case of mistaken identity. That would be of interest."

"Okay, Leslie, how do you unravel that?"

"I was beginning to think about how a sniper could mistakenly pick an innocent victim. My first thought was name confusion. He killed the wrong Dolph Leonard."

"I assume that's why you have those telephone directories on your desk. Can I be of any assistance, Ms. Nugent?"

"Sure. Why don't you work on the Manhattan directory while I dig into the Bronx?"

Ten minutes later they had identified a total of four Dolph and Adolph Leonards, two in the Bronx and two in Manhattan. They agreed on a script for a call and each took several numbers. One was the actual shooting victim. The address saved them that embarrassing call. One was an elderly widower living in a rest home. Another was a young actor currently in an out-of-town production of *Damn Yankees*. His roommate indicated that he'd been out on the West Coast for two months. Gentle questioning revealed that the actor had no political interests whatsoever. The last Leonard was a dancer in the Alvin Alley troop.

"Looks like a dry well to me, Leslie."

"I agree. Let's try a different spelling. Try 'Lenard.'"

There was one Dolph Lenard in the Bronx directory. Google had some information on him. He was a strong supporter of white supremacy causes, contributing letters frequently and articles occasionally to neo-Nazi newspapers. His contributions had earned him a spot on Google.

"Okay, Gary, here's my scenario. Shooter X is looking for a victim. He discovers Dolph Lenard in some hate-filled newspaper but erroneously writes down Dolph Leonard in a not-so-legible scrawl. When he looks up his address in the Bronx phone book he encounters only two Dolph Leonards. One is easily eliminated because he's in a home for the aged. That leaves our victim. The sniper tracks him down and ends his life with two shots in the back." Leslie looked up with an expression that said, "Whadda you think?"

Gary was thinking it through. "It's possible. We'll never know. It does give credence to the notion that the sniper killed the wrong person. It also explains why the police can't find a motive for the killing. It also doesn't match our sniper's M.O. This sniper was careless and our sniper is meticulous. Makes me think there's a new sniper on the block."

"Exactly what I was thinking. The bullets don't match either. I'm going to give Lionel Cobb a call and see if he buys it.

CHAPTER FORTY-FOUR

The short story in *The Times* noting the shooting in the Bronx was buried in the pages covering local news. *The Bronx Home News* gave it greater coverage for a day, but in the absence of any motive, suspects, or interesting background information the story was short-lived.

Bert Alder was an interested reader. He was sure the police were thinking "sniper" but didn't utter the word, absent any leads in that direction. He wondered what that lady reporter made of it. She was smart. Very smart. He was sure she'd have doubts about the sniper being responsible.

Terry read the coverage and agreed with Bert that the police were holding back. The previous night she'd slept over in Bert's apartment and could vouch for his not being involved in the killing. Her suspicion about his identity as the sniper was fast fading. If the police had attributed the latest killing to the sniper that would have ended it. So, faint doubt lingered in her mind.

Henry Gold was another interested reader. He wondered why the police weren't screaming "sniper" and adding this kill to the list of sniper hits. Something was missing here. There was no mention of a hate crime or of the victim's neo-Nazi leanings. The coverage was terse and revealed nothing of unusual interest. He was puzzled, but he was determined to go on and find another victim with virulent anti-Semitic "credentials."

Gold's family had been decimated in the Holocaust. His young father and even younger mother had escaped by the skin of their teeth. Henry was born to them late in their marriage. Now, in his mid-sixties, he made regular trips to the Jewish cemetery where both were buried. His older sister, Sarah, was buried alongside them.

The recent news from his doctor had been devastating. He had advanced colon cancer and would likely live only a year or two more. Taking some Jew-hating bigots with him to the grave seemed like a fitting end to his life. His wife, Toby, knew he was dying. Together they had made their peace with his fate. Their two children were well along in their careers and family lives. His decision to find solace on a vengeful path was not shared with anyone.

A third person took an interest in the killing. Ernst Cummings was surprised at the paucity of information in the newspaper coverage. Although the shooting had some hallmarks of the sniper shootings in the past, there was one disparate feature. When he inquired, no one in the neo-Nazi community knew anything about the victim. That was more than just odd. All previous victims were known to that tight knit community.

To Cummings it suggested the target was a mistake. The sniper's first mistake. He concentrated on this finding. An alternative explanation intrigued him. It might mean a new sniper had entered the game and this one was not as fastidious as the other. Two targets would justify double his agreed-upon fee, but he doubted the organizations of neo-Nazis in the metropolitan area could raise that kind of money.

Cummings was relaxing in his luxury condominium high up in Trump Towers. His well-known art dealership was profitable but not sufficient to support the lifestyle he afforded himself. He needed a luxurious apartment and enjoyed the expansive cultural opportunities in Manhattan. He also enjoyed the female companionship that visible wealth attracted. At forty-four he found his other source of income essential.

When Eric Voight explained the assignment to him he thought it an easy case to take on and readily accepted the generous fee. As he thought about it, the challenge was more daunting than he had imagined. Killing the sniper was hardly a problem, but *catching* the sniper was going to take some imaginative trap setting. Now though he probably had two targets and the newcomer might be less of a problem. He'd give it some serious thought tomorrow.

Tonight his companion deserved his full attention. He could feel his organ beginning to harden as he remembered how she introduced herself to him at the opera intermission two weeks ago. His date had gone to the powder room. The lobby was so crowded it was difficult to find any floor space not already occupied. Toni used the crowding to good advantage and put a hand firmly on his ass. She introduced herself by voice as well and thus began a torrid affair that continued into the present.

Cummings was a boyish-looking six-footer with curly brown hair combed loosely. Two decades ago he was a first-string soccer player with Liverpool but wasn't a star. He maintained his athlete's physical condition with regular workouts but had put on twenty pounds in recent years. Women found him appealing and he knew how to make them feel desired. Throw in an art dealership for panache, along with a considerable income, and it was easy to see why he found life so gratifying. Being a paid assassin was only a means to an end, the end being that income he so enjoyed. Pampered as a child and highly successful throughout his school years, he never developed any restraining moral code. Living well was his inclination, killing was his avocation.

CHAPTER FORTY-FIVE

Henry Gold wasn't finding it difficult to identify candidates for killing. A Google search for neo-Nazi groups was very helpful. It led him to the Southern Poverty Law Center and there he learned about the numerous hate groups in New York State, a number of which resided in New York City itself. From this resource he culled the names of several prominent players in the hate game. He settled on one particularly outspoken leader and again used Google to locate him. His work for this week would entail observing his quarry and deciding when and where to hit him.

Since his diagnosis was made he'd gone on extended leave from his accounting practice. His partners were sympathetic and afforded him whatever time he needed to clear up the loose ends in his life. He was grateful for their forbearance. His work colleagues were a part of his life he felt sorrowful about leaving behind.

His chosen target owned a tattoo parlor in a marginal area of the south-central Bronx. His name was Larry Xander, thirty-eight years old, unmarried and sporting a wide variety of tattoos on his arms, neck, and back. He was a walking billboard for his business. His most popular tattoo was a Star of David made up of dollar bills.

Henry scouted the area around the parlor for a good location. He also followed Xander home to his apartment just ten blocks away and again looked around for a good site to shoot from. The tattoo parlor did much of its work in the evenings and didn't close up until after 10:00 p.m. Xander was the last one to leave the parlor and usually walked home. Henry identified a spot several blocks from Xander's apartment. It was a mostly empty, small parking lot with a good view of the street Xander walked to get home. His plan was complete.

Ernst Cummings had mapped out a strategy to nab the sniper. It was complex and needed a large number of volunteers to enact it. He played the odds. If it didn't work he'd try something else. Each killing might yield some information leading him closer to the sniper. Most of the sniper killings had taken place in the Bronx with the exception of the Staten Island killing.

He decided to place watchers in areas of the Bronx that looked to him like possible shooting locations. The watcher idea had been suggested to him by Voight when he was hired. He enlisted twenty-five men from various sympathetic groups and assigned the men, singly, to vantage points he selected. The watchers would be on duty from dusk until midnight.

In the event of a shooting, nearby watchers would converge on the area and identify any possible suspects. He was not planning on *preventing* a shooting. That was not possible. He was hoping the sniper would operate in or near one of the areas he'd chosen and then make the mistake of trying to leave in a manner raising the suspicion of one of his watchers. The watcher would follow the suspect and stay in phone contact with Cummings until the latter could catch up and take over. More likely, the suspect would leave the area in a car. The watcher would try to photograph the car for subsequent license plate identification. Cummings told the watchers that he would pay $5,000 for a license plate photo that led to the capture or killing of the shooter.

For five nights there was no shooting. Cummings had to keep the watchers on their toes and not let them get too bored with their assignment. On night six the sniper struck. Xander was taken down on his walk home at approximately 11:00 p.m. Two shots, one to the head and one to the chest, were fatal. A watcher three blocks away heard the shots and headed in the direction the noise came from. When he turned a corner and entered the street where he could see a body lying on the sidewalk, a car drove past him in the opposite direction at a relatively fast speed. As instructed, he stopped whatever he was doing and took a cellphone picture of the car as it drove away.

Cummings arrived at the scene ten minutes later in his car. The two men went over to the fallen victim and confirmed that he was dead. The watcher called 911 and gave his phone and phone ID to Cummings. Cummings was surprised the network of watchers had worked as well as it did. Serendipity was a great ally, he thought. The photo would tell him just how successful or unsuccessful it was. There was no certainty that the car photographed had anything to do with the shooting. On the other hand there had been very few cars on the street in that area at that late hour.

Henry Gold drove home, satisfied that he'd accomplished something of meaning. He had made good use of his time and looked forward to the morning newspaper and any news of the killing. He was still surprised that his first killing hadn't been linked to the sniper. This time he was sure it would be different. The victim tonight was a highly visible figure in the hate community.

The photo on the watcher's phone was of low quality when it was blown up.

At the distance it was shot it required considerable enlargement to be of value. Nevertheless, the license plate details could be made out and, with sophisticated photo enhancement programs, could be read with reasonable certainty. Cummings called a colleague in the Department of Motor Vehicles whose name was given to him by Midler. The friendly clerk looked up the owner of that plate and passed his name on to Cummings within a matter of minutes. Henry Gold's address was a bonus.

CHAPTER FORTY-SIX

The late night street shooting of a known neo-Nazi had "sniper" written all over it. Lionel Cobb noted that the bullets matched those extracted from the body of Dolph Leonard. He had no doubt that both were the work of a sniper. But, once again, there were no clues at the shooting site to help identify the shooter. Leslie commiserated with the lieutenant about their inability to get any traction in this case. She could only hope the sniper would call and possibly clear up the mystery about a second sniper. Hope was all she had.

Henry Gold lived with his wife in an apartment in the Riverdale section of the Bronx. Cummings visited the apartment house, identified the Gold apartment, and staked it out. He knew Henry's wife, Toby, left for work around 3:00 p.m. for the evening nursing shift at Montefiore Hospital.

Shortly after six, Cummings knocked on the door of the apartment. Gold opened it without asking any questions. Cummings forced his way in and pushed Gold onto the floor. He pointed his pistol at the stunned man and told him to stay down.

"Just stay where you are and you won't get hurt. I'm not here to rob you. I just want you to answer some questions for me."

Gold was puzzled. He never saw the man before and had never had a gun pointed at him. He was speechless.

"I know you shot and killed a man last night. Don't ask how I know, I just do. I want to know if you shot a man named Dolph Leonard over a week ago."

Gold hesitated but quickly realized this man knew about his sniper activity. He also was not likely to be bluffed or fooled by any evasive answers.

"Yes, I did," was all he offered.

"Now for the hard part. Why did you kill Leonard?"

"For the same reason I shot Xander two nights ago. I hate neo-Nazis."

"Why did you think Leonard was a neo-Nazi? None of the local Jew-hater crowd ever heard of him. He was not a neo-Nazi."

"He was. I read about him in those hate papers. He was a neo-Nazi and deserved to die. I have the papers over there on the table. If you let me get up I'll show you."

"Okay. Show me. But be careful, I won't hesitate to use this gun."

Gold got up from the floor and went over to the dining room table where there was a pile of newspapers. He pulled one out of the pile and handed it to Cummings.

"You can find his article on the front page."

Cummings scanned the page. He smiled.

"You fool. You killed an innocent man. You killed Dolph Leonard. The man you wanted to kill is Dolph Lenard. That's Lenard, spelled without an 'o.' Somehow you screwed up. That explains why the police haven't tied that killing to the sniper killings. It has no tie-in."

"Let me see the paper. I don't believe you." He was handed the paper and sobbed as he read it and realized his mistake.

120

"Now, what about all those other sniper killings? Did you do any of them?"

"No. My first was the 'wrong man killing.' Xander was my second. That's all I've done. I swear."

Cummings was satisfied. There was nothing more to gain here. He was getting paid to kill the real sniper. The original. Not this bumbling guy. He saw no reason to kill Gold. He killed for money and there was no price on this guy's head.

"You're a lucky guy, Mr. Gold. I'm giving you a pass. But with this warning: you're out of the sniper game permanently. Do you understand? I just retired you. Stay retired and you'll never see me again. Are we in agreement?"

Henry Gold realized he'd been given a second life, albeit a rather short one. He nodded in agreement. Cummings put his gun away and left the apartment.

CHAPTER FORTY-SEVEN

The sniper killing of Larry Xander was all the proof Terry Alder needed to be finally convinced Bert was not the sniper. They had spent every night together for the past week and this exonerated him.

She called her friend Diane and, in the course of the conversation, admitted that her suspicion about Bert had been proven foolish. Diane had been right to be skeptical. They had a good laugh.

Diane suggested they meet for lunch to catch up on each other's lives. She mentioned a friend she'd bring along if Terry didn't mind.

"I think you'll like her. She has a good sense of humor and is a straight shooter. She's a reporter at *The Times* named Leslie Nugent. You may have seen her byline on the spate of recent stories covering the sniper shootings. She brings some real smarts to the table."

"I recognize the name. I think I met her at a hospital bash. Now I remember; it was the pediatric department annual party. She was with some new anesthesiologist. Bert was with me. I caught him checking her out. He thought I didn't notice. She and I had a pleasant chat about something. Doctors' wives, if I recall."

"So, what did you think, Terry?"

"Pleasant enough. A real good-looker, too. Bert had reason to look her over."

"She's single and straight, Terry. When you meet her you'll wonder how she managed to remain single so long. She called me after that party and suggested the three of us meet for lunch. I gave her the okay but it never happened. She probably forgot. Now, I'm going to make up for that lapse. I'll text you with a time and place.

"In the meantime, I'd like to borrow your car this afternoon to do a few household errands. I won't need it for more than a few hours and should have it back by five o'clock at the latest. Is that okay?"

"Sure, Diane. I have no need for the car today, so keep it as long as you need to. Bert and I share the car, much as we did before the divorce, and rarely have any need for it."

"Thanks. Talk to you soon."

Diane's errands took her to a big supermarket in Queens. She did her food shopping and picked up a few household necessities. She loaded them on the back seat and headed home. She looked forward to a quiet supper of soup and Korean deep-fried wings, the latter a specialty of the market. A large black decaf coffee sat in the console with a loosely affixed lid.

Waiting at a light shortly after entering Manhattan over the Queensboro Bridge, Diane was jolted by the car behind her. She got out to survey any damage to the rear end of her borrowed car. A dent in the bumper was the only bruise and it was very modest in degree. The driver of the offending vehicle was apologetic and offered to pay for any repairs. They exchanged insurance information and driver's license information. Diane said she would file an accident report with the police to satisfy the insurance companies.

When she walked back to the car she saw her much anticipated supper spilled all over the back seat. The soup and wings were a disaster.

A man who witnessed the accident offered to serve as a witness if he was needed. She took his phone number. He then told her that two blocks from there was a carwash and he bet they would do a very professional cleanup of her car's interior. Again she thanked him, got in the car, and drove over to Sim's Carwash.

A crew of three men went to work on the car's interior. Diane sat in a waiting area where a large supply of *People's Magazine* helped her pass the time. One of the workers—"Carlos" said his sewn-on name piece—stood before her trying to get her attention. She put aside the story on Kim Kardashian and followed him to the car. The rear seat had been removed to get at any soup that had seeped between the seat cushion and the back of the seat. Diane could see what had caught his attention. With the seat cushion removed, a rifle was plainly seen on the floor. Carlos said the men didn't want to touch it and he was just calling it to her attention. Diane was stunned, but she recovered quickly and told the men to finish cleaning and just replace the cushion.

Her mind was spinning. She paid for the cleaning and gave the trio very generous tips. She drove a very clean car out of the carwash. Diane drove to her apartment house, unloaded the bundles with the help of the doorman, brought them up to her apartment, and stored the contents. She then returned the car to Terry's parking place, still unsure what to do with her new information.

She doubted that her friend was aware of the rifle. Terry was so happy to see Bert exonerated as the sniper that she considered the matter closed. Diane was unsure how to proceed.

CHAPTER FORTY-EIGHT

The weekly television news show *It's Happening Now* was put together two weeks in advance. The group that planned each program met in the conference room in the network's office space in midtown Manhattan. The planners were Hal Newcome, the program's creator, now its producer; Jock Deverow, the program's director; Michael Owens, the creative coordinator; and Lowell Somers, the moderator of the show.

Newcome ran the meeting but it was a free-for-all. He threw his idea out on the table and stood back.

"The sniper is as hot as any subject and there haven't been any high profile shows wrestling with the issues it raises." Newcome had the group's attention.

Deverow was first to respond. "This subject has been on our collective minds for some time, Hal. Trouble is, without an identified sniper it loses a lot of its appeal. If there was a way to have the sniper agree to be a call-in guest on the program it would ignite a lot of listener interest. I just don't see it happening though."

Owens chimed in, "We could set up the program and before it runs, ask the sniper to call in on a disposable phone and say whatever he wants to. I know we don't have his phone number, but *The Times* was able to get him to respond to their open letter. He can be reached."

Newcome was warming to the idea. "I like the format of the sniper watching the show and commenting whenever he feels like it. I don't think it'll be difficult to put together a panel. The question is whether we stick our necks out, gambling on the sniper calling in. I think we'd have to low-key that aspect of the program. If he calls in, great! If not, we didn't promise a sniper interview.

"If we can get that *Times* reporter who spoke to him on the phone, that might work in our favor. He saw her as a good listener who didn't try to trick him into revealing his identity. She'd be a real plus." Newcome was searching for her name. "Nugent. That's it. Leslie Nugent. I can feel the program coming together. Mike, will you take a shot on bringing Ms. Nugent on board?"

"Sure, Hal. Shouldn't be too difficult."

"Okay then. It's taking shape for two weeks forward. I'm getting excited." Hal Newcome scanned the faces in the room, soliciting questions and comments. "I want each of you to submit two questions to me that will address the subject on air. Also, any bright ideas you come up with in the interim, just text me."

CHAPTER FORTY-NINE

November was the month for Jews to commemorate Kristallnacht, the Night of Broken Glass. This was a pogrom carried out by paramilitary Nazis across Germany in 1938. It targeted Jewish homes and businesses, breaking windows, ransacking business, burning synagogues, arresting and beating Jews. Law enforcement personnel and firefighters stood by and offered no protection to the Jews or their property. To commemorate the atrocity, a rally was scheduled in Prospect Park, Brooklyn. A few short speeches would be followed by a music program.

In spite of a light drizzle, a huge crowd turned out. Security was high but the turnout made it difficult to screen packages, bags, and backpacks the way the police would have liked. Midway through the speeches a bomb was detonated in a crowded area of the audience. Ten people were killed and a dozen more wounded. No one could be implicated on site in the killing. The bomb was a homemade affair, leaving no clues for the police or FBI.

Bert and Terry were just leaving the theater at Lincoln Center when news of the attack began to spread through the streets. Bert clenched his teeth but didn't want to show any visible signs of his anger. Terry hugged him close to her and cried softly. People in the street were visibly angry. Some were shouting anti-Nazi epithets. Bert picked up the story on his iPhone and confirmed the news

It had been two months since he stopped shooting. In the interim there had been no Nazi attacks. He'd hoped that his shooting had lessened the likelihood of an attack like tonight's but he had no illusion they wouldn't continue. The other sniper had launched one or maybe two reprisals, but that too had abated.

He was conflicted. He wanted to continue his new relationship with Terry but didn't see how he could resume shooting and still maintain his innocence in her eyes. He felt an uncontrollable anger that triggered a powerful urge to respond to this latest attack. The attack had been like giving a drink to a recovering alcoholic. He'd have to find a way to retaliate.

CHAPTER FIFTY

The carnage in Prospect Park was hideous. TV coverage was extensive on all local networks. It resembled the Boston Marathon bombing. Many of the survivors were severely injured, including loss of limbs.

Leslie and Gary, like most New Yorkers, were glued to the television set. Leslie's cell phone rang. At this late hour a phone call was not likely to be good news. She didn't recognize the caller's name but answered anyway.

"Leslie Nugent here."

"This is Michael Owens, Ms. Nugent. I work at WNYC on the TV side. I need a few minutes of your time. Is it okay to talk now?"

"I guess so, Mr. Owens. What's so important that you had to call at this late hour? And on this most disturbing night?"

"Well, the madness in Brooklyn is related to my reason for calling. Hear me out. I'm the creative coordinator on *It's Happening Now*, our popular weekly news magazine. We're planning a panel program in two weeks discussing aspects of the sniper issue. We'd like to have you sit on the panel along with representatives from law enforcement, the mayor's office, and a major national Jewish organization. The program is very much in the early planning stage so I can't give you any details.

"Ideally, we'd have the sniper comment on various issues raised by the panel. Our planners noted that you had actually spoken with the sniper and thought you might have some thoughts on how to bring him into the discussion. I'll stop here."

"I didn't want interrupt you, Mr. Owens, so I let you finish your spiel. I'd be happy to participate but I warn you that I don't have access to the sniper. He's very careful not to reveal any data about himself and won't be tricked into doing so. If he senses this is a trap of any kind, he'll just turn us off.

"Having said that, I'm curious to learn what the objective of the program is. Good people with backgrounds in mental health have opined regarding the psyche of this man. I doubt he'd be likely to reveal much in that vein even if we were lucky enough to have him call in to the program. He's already stated his position. The atrocity tonight can only reinforce his position and may start him shooting again. One last thing, you may want to put a member of the neo-Nazi community on the panel. That would heat up the show considerably. I also think a psychiatrist should be added in place of the mayor's representative."

"I can see that you'll be an invaluable member of the panel, Ms. Nugent. I'll think about your suggestions. I'm looking forward to meeting you. I'll contact you about a planning session as soon as one is scheduled. Thanks for your time. I mean it."

Leslie put down her phone and turned to Gary.

"Well, Gary, I just launched my career as a TV journalist. That was WNYC putting me on a panel for a program dealing with the sniper."

"Good luck, Leslie. I thought you were getting stale as a print journalist. Time to branch out and capitalize on your good looks."

CHAPTER FIFTY-ONE

Herman Midler was growing increasingly impatient. There'd been no word from Voight's man about progress in eliminating the sniper. Now, with the incident in Brooklyn, the sniper was likely to come back to life after a quiet period. No telling where he'd direct his anger. He called Voight.

"Yes, Herman, I do understand your concern. Trouble is, during the peaceful period that just ended there was no sniper activity for my man to focus on. Now, that recent event will probably draw the sniper out. Our man will get to work and seek out his target. Just think of the Brooklyn attack as baiting the trap."

Midler was mollified although apprehensive about his safety and that of his men.

Leslie met with Lionel Cobb to jointly contemplate the new landscape in view of the recent mass killing.

"There's nothing new to report, but I suspect we're on the verge of renewed sniper activity. We've instituted some new surveillance. We now fly our police helicopters over the Bronx at night, concentrating on an area that encompasses the past sniper shootings. If he decides to expand his perimeter we'll be out of luck, but we'll just reconfigure the coverage area to encompass the new crime scene. We've increased patrols in that area, so if the helicopters see anything suspicious the patrols can be alerted and arrive on scene a bit faster. I know it sounds thin but we're doing the best we can with limited information."

"Don't be defeatist, Lionel. I think something will break and these tools may turn out to be good measures to have on hand. I have something to ask you that's a bit of a sidestep. There's going to be a TV program focused on the sniper. I've been asked to be on the panel and I wonder if you'd be interested in serving as the spokesperson for law enforcement. I warn you, it puts you on the spot since there's been no tangible progress shown by law enforcement. You'll draw some angry criticism if they take calls, as I think they will."

"Count me in, Leslie. If I get an invitation I'll join the party."

Ernst Cummings reflected on the aftermath of the deadly explosion. For him it breathed new life into his hunting effort. The success of his watcher program in nailing the second shooter encouraged him to put it in place again and hope for another lucky encounter.

CHAPTER FIFTY-TWO

The moon was in the crescent phase. It shed little light at this late hour. The drive out to Queens was not encumbered by any traffic. Bert had chosen a target outside of his usual hunting ground. He was concerned that he'd developed a pattern in his shootings and felt it wise to mix up areas he exploited.

The smell in the car bothered him. It had the odor of cleaning fluid and indeed the car interior was exceptionally clean. He couldn't account for the surprising condition of the seat covers. He'd ask Terry about this in the morning. Tonight she'd decided to sleep in her own apartment where she had to catch up on domestic matters such as laundry, purging the refrigerator of dated foods, and doing some light cleaning. Bert took advantage of her absence to resume his sniper activity.

He was in a neighborhood new to him, but with the GPS it was easy to find his way to The Grill Palace, a popular neighborhood restaurant owned by Bernard Loftus. Loftus was a leadership figure in the America for Americans chapter in Queens. His occasional anti-Semitic rant on Instagram labeled him as a prime target for the sniper.

The restaurant was on a dead-end street with a small park at the street's end. The only other building on the street was an auto repair shop that closed at six. Bert was parked up the street at the entrance to the dead end. The restaurant's parking lot was almost empty so he anticipated that closing time was fast approaching. The few cars on the street probably belonged to the staff. He had no way to identify Loftus's car.

The loaded rifle lay in his lap. He'd noted how clean the area under the back seat was. No question that the car had been professionally cleaned. In that process, someone would have seen the rifle. He was mildly disturbed about this development but forced himself to stay focused on the reason he was here in Queens.

The parking lot was empty except for one car, a recent model BMW. Bert was betting that car belonged to Loftus. Three people, a man and two women, exited the restaurant and its lights were turned off. The two women got into the remaining car on the street and were quick to leave, taking no notice of his car. That left no witnesses to be concerned about. The man headed to the BMW. Bert was sure he had his target. He quickly sighted on the man and dispatched him with a single shot to the head before he could get into his car.

Bert left Queens feeling satisfied. This had been a simple assassination. He'd remember to remove the stolen license plate covering his own plate once he was back at the outdoor parking spot behind the building he and Terry had lived in together. He then cabbed over to his apartment. He decided to take the rifle inside, so he broke it down into its two parts and carried it inside in a shopping bag. Tomorrow he'd replace it under the seat with the old pellet rifle he'd had forever; a vestige of his childhood that he never threw away. He and Terry called it "Rosebud" after the sled in *Citizen Kane*.

Realizing that someone probably saw the rifle under the seat during the cleaning, he decided to get rid of it. If for any reason the police came looking for his rifle they'd find the old pellet gun under the seat and no rifle in his apartment. Better safe than sorry.

CHAPTER FIFTY-THREE

It was a perfect day for outdoor dining and there was no more outdoorsy restaurant than Tavern on the Green in Central Park. Diane and Leslie had Ubered over together and now waited for Terry before they could be seated.

"I finally got our trio together, Leslie. It wasn't easy finding a lunch hour time that satisfied each of us. Do you remember, you called me after some hospital party? I told you I knew Terry at Sarah Lawrence. We were two years apart and only casual acquaintances at the time. When we met up again years later, our friendship took hold and developed into a close relationship. Now, we talk several times a week and try to do lunch every two weeks or so. She recently divorced her husband of many years but now they seem to have rekindled their romance."

"I met them both at that party, Diane. And I do remember calling you about it that night."

Diane pointed to the door and indicated that Terry had just arrived. They exchanged warm greetings and were led to their table by a young woman in a well-tailored suit.

Terry was in a talkative, effusive mood whereas Diane seemed subdued. Leslie took this in and wondered why Diane had withdrawn as soon as her good friend arrived on the scene. Up until that moment she seemed upbeat and pleased about the luncheon she'd set up.

Leslie tried to pick up the mood where Diane had let it falter.

"I understand you're a paralegal, Terry. Is that the career you got into right out of college?"

"Yes it is, Leslie. I might have gone on to law school but my husband and I needed an income while he completed his pediatric training. Law school seemed an expensive undertaking while paralegal training was a quicker, less costly alternative. I probably thought I'd get around to law school eventually but that just never happened. I like my work and think I do a good job. How about you, Leslie?"

Leslie responded without hesitation. "The career part is pretty straightforward for me, Terry. I've been a newspaper reporter all my working life. I worked at a small paper in northern Virginia for ten years before I broke a big story about the president and received a job offer from *The Times*. That's about it. I love reporting and *The Times* has given me a lot of latitude in what I cover. I couldn't ask for a better job."

The two women listening to Leslie sat silent for a moment, each contemplating this rather appealing younger woman who seemed to have it all. Terry wanted to hear more about her personal life since there was no ring on her left hand. In a noncompetitive way she was looking for some flaw. She decided to be frank. "No engagement ring, Leslie. How have you managed to stay single with what you have going for you?"

Leslie smiled at Terry's direct approach. "I'm the one usually asking the probing questions but I'm willing to go further with my story. I'm single and live alone. I've had my share of serious romantic entanglements but haven't been to the altar. I'm seeing a guy now and thinking long term, but we're not rushing it. I know I'm very eligible but inside the cover of this book is a woman with the usual concerns about marriage, family, and career. People underestimate my determination to succeed at my career. There's no 'trophy wife' lurking here waiting for a billionaire hedge fund guy to carry her off." She paused. "Hey, that's enough about me."

Diane was smiling and nodding her head up and down.

Terry just stared at Leslie, and finally responded, "I asked a simple question and you came back with a penetrating answer I can only admire for its insight and honesty. Thanks, Leslie."

The lunch progressed with a lot of small talk about theatre and museums.

Diane asked Terry if she'd been following Leslie's stories on the sniper.

"Who doesn't, Diane? Leslie, you seem to have outdistanced your competition on this story. What can you tell us that's not on the front page yet?"

"Well, WNYC has put together a panel for its news magazine show this Sunday, devoting the full hour to the sniper story. I'm one of five panelists. Our outside hope is that the sniper might call in to comment. He's been remarkably clever about covering his tracks and remaining a total secret."

Diane asked, "Who makes up the panel, Les?"

"Without naming names, we have a reporter, me, a law enforcement person, a psychiatrist, a representative of a large Jewish organization, and a representative of the America for Americans organization. I hope we can maintain a collegial atmosphere and answer questions phoned in by listeners. This issue has divided the community in a way we hadn't envisioned. The sniper isn't alone on the issue he raised during his phone conversations with me."

Terry asked the next logical question, "Where do *you* stand on that issue, Leslie? Does a reporter have to assume a neutral position to cover the story in an evenhanded manner?"

"Hey, guys, I opened up about my personal life, but now you're invading my professional life. That's even more private."

The group was unsure where to go next with sniper talk.

Leslie thought it necessary to reassure her friends that they hadn't crossed over some sensitive line. "I'm only kidding. I find the sniper's position *almost* defensible. He sees a war going on and has taken the side of the Jews. He's out there all alone because a supportive public is unwilling or unable go all the way with his position. I guess that's where I stand."

Diane was visibly anxious about something.

"Leslie, please forgive me for including you in a discussion I have to have with Terry. We could take it outside or wait for you to leave but I don't see any harm in letting you hear what I have to say. You've been very up front with us so I count you in as a friend to both of us."

"What the hell are you talking about, Diane?" was Terry's expression of surprise.

"Okay, hear me out. Terry, remember when you were suspicious that Bert, your ex, might actually *be* the sniper? I told you that was crazy but you went on to check out the shooting dates against your schedule of late nights at work.

They jibed, you may recall, and it wasn't until a shooting occurred on a night that Bert spent with you that you were convinced of the absurdity of your suspicion. Remember, you initially thought Bert might be the sniper based on a conversation you had with him after his mother's funeral?

"Last week, I borrowed your car and did some household shopping. On the way home the car was gently rear-ended. No structural damage but my foodstuffs in the back seat were knocked over and spilled all over the seat. I took the car to a carwash and had the interior professionally cleaned. The cleaners removed the rear seat to clean it and discovered a rifle under the seat. They had me see the rifle before they replaced the seat. That's my story. Now I'm wondering that maybe you weren't such a nut job after all."

Leslie found this intriguing. This simple, friendly luncheon seemed to go in a variety of directions.

Terry was speechless. Leslie felt uncomfortably like an outsider who had walked in on a very personal conversation between two friends. That didn't stop her mind from turning over the information before her. She held her tongue.

Diane was aware of the mood swing she'd created and tried to breathe some life back into the group.

"Hey, guys, I didn't mean to break up the party. I apologize to you, Leslie, for bringing you into this personal matter without any preparation. That was unfair."

Terry was recovered and ready with her response.

"Ladies, as we wind up this whirlwind luncheon, let me suggest that we cab over to my car, lift the seat, and look at the damn rifle."

"Great idea. Leslie, are you coming with us?"

"Wouldn't miss this for anything. Let's go."

The threesome got into a cab and was standing alongside Terry's parked car in fifteen minutes. Terry unlocked the car and commented on the cleaning fluid smell and the very clean interior. They lifted the rear seat and saw the rifle.

"Looks like something no self-respecting sniper would use to commit eight murders." Leslie's droll comment brought some nervous laughter from the other two women. She cautioned them not to touch it and advised Terry to leave it in place.

Terry finally spoke up. "This is a pellet gun Bert has treasured since childhood and would never let me dispose of. We nicknamed it Rosebud. Looks like he wanted to appease me by getting it out of the house and burying it here in our car."

Leslie had a question. "Does it look like the rifle you saw last week, Diane?"

"Can't say with any certainty. Wish I had a better visual recollection."

Terry thought this had been the most bizarre luncheon she'd ever been to. She apologized to Leslie for probing her private life and then taking her on this wild goose chase. "All our lunch dates aren't this stressful,

Leslie. I hope you'll dare to join us again and experience a more normal luncheon."

Terry hugged Diane and flashed her a smile. She then headed into her apartment building while Leslie and Diane walked a bit before hailing a cab.

"Diane, can you remember where you had the car cleaned?"

"I knew it, Leslie. You weren't about to let that story rest. It was Sim's Carwash somewhere on the Upper Eastside and it was a guy named Carlos who wanted me to see the rifle."

Leslie pursued the matter with Diane. "Did you see the rifle in a good light? Was there a telescopic sight on it? In other words, do you recall any identifying features?"

Diane tried to be responsive but, in truth, she hadn't looked very closely at the rifle. "I can't offer any useful information. It was a rifle. That's all."

Leslie grabbed a cab and headed off to Sim's.

It wasn't hard to find. The cabby knew exactly where it was. Carlos wasn't hard to find either. At first he was cautious about answering any questions, but a ten-dollar bill eased his anxiety.

"Carlos, do you remember a car interior you cleaned last week? You cleaned the seats for a woman who had spilled some food on them. You removed the rear seat and saw something you wanted the woman to see. Can you to describe what it was?"

Leslie stopped here and looked at Carlos with some intensity.

"I saw a gun on the floor under the seat. I didn't touch it. I don't know why I wanted her to see it but I was being extra careful. I guess I didn't want her to think we took anything from that hiding place."

"Carlos, describe the gun to me as best you can."

"I'm not a gun guy. But this rifle looked pretty good to me. It was very clean and looked almost like new. It had one of those telescope sights on it. That's all I can tell you."

"Thanks, Carlos. That's very helpful."

She slipped him another ten spot and left.

CHAPTER FIFTY-FOUR

Gary was devouring his favorite dinner and Leslie wasn't far behind him. Not being Jewish didn't stop her from frying up lox, onions, and eggs and enjoying it as much as her Jewish guy. Toasted bagels were essential and Gary insisted on scallion cream cheese. Leslie didn't want to change the mood of the meal so she kept silent on the matter of the sniper until Gary's plate was clean.

"I've got something to bat around with you, Gary. It's important that I have your full attention."

"Leslie, out with it. I'm all yours."

"I had an interesting lunch today with Diane and Terry Alder. Diane reminded Terry that she, Terry, had once suspected her ex-husband of being the sniper. Eventually she exonerated him because she could vouch for his presence with her on one night the sniper did his deed. I didn't bring up the issue that we were suspicious that a second sniper was

141

possibly responsible for that kill. That would have left her husband in sniper limbo. Are you following me so far?"

"I'm all ears, Leslie. I know we're just coming to the good part."

"Bear with me, Gary. It gets a lot deeper. Moving on, Diane told a story I won't repeat that ended up with her seeing a rifle hidden under the back seat of Terry's car. Actually, she and Bert share the car. Getting warm? The three of us went to see the rifle and found an old pellet gun under the seat. It was an old treasured relic from Bert's childhood. Diane couldn't describe the rifle she'd seen only fleetingly at a carwash. Terry thought this finding again exonerated her ex. She floated away on a cloud back to her apartment. I didn't mention this, but Terry and her ex are back together, and in love. Anyway, the story doesn't end here.

"This intrepid reporter went back to the carwash where Diane had seen the rifle. Carlos, the man who cleaned the backseat and discovered the rifle, was at work and responded to a ten-dollar bill by describing a rifle very different than the one we three ladies saw in Terry's car. He described a very new-looking rifle with a telescopic sight. To quote Carlos, 'the rifle looked pretty good to me.' Trust me, Gary, it wasn't the rifle I saw in Terry's car."

"Quite a story, Leslie. Let me prove how closely I listened. The owner of the rifle realized the seat had been cleaned and surmised that someone may have seen the rifle. So, clever sniper that he is, he replaces the rifle with one that has no material value to the police in identifying its owner as the sniper. He stays one step ahead of everyone except my dogged journalist friend who went back to the carwash. Quite a teaching moment to share with some young cub reporter. Trouble is there's no hard evidence to identify the sniper. What you have is Carlos's verbal description of the gun and even that is somewhat incomplete. What strikes me as compelling is the owner switching guns. Still though, no hard evidence. It leaves *you* as the only person who knows the sniper's identity. This may help you in your coverage of the mystery, I think. Next step, talk to your policeman friend, Lionel Cobb.

"But one more thing, Leslie. You're getting close to the sniper so a warning is in order. He kills for a reason, but he kills, nevertheless. Don't be lulled into complacency by his clearly stated philosophy. *He* defines the enemy and *he* can broaden his definition to include anyone he places in that camp. If threatened by discovery he might define any person who could uncover him as one of the enemy; a person seeking to end his shooting and spare Nazis. He is a killer. Don't forget that."

"That's helpful, Gary. And I do appreciate your warning."

For Leslie, life with Gary was growing increasingly comfortable. He was a partner in the true sense of the word. They communed on stories, enjoyed the same jokes, and seemed to understand each other's concerns before they expressed them. The relationship defined compatibility. Beyond that though, his intelligence and insights were invaluable and added a dimension to their relationship that went beyond just compatibility.

CHAPTER FIFTY-FIVE

Buying a handgun from a private party is easy if you scan the right online message boards. Bert scanned the ads on several hate web-sites and picked out one that offered a used M9 Beretta, a standard army sidearm. Since he only wanted it for a one-time use he was only concerned about reliability, and that was what the Beretta was known for. He made the buy.

The business card tucked behind the car visor on the passenger side advertised Sim's Carwash, offering one free wash after nine washes. He safely assumed this was where his car had been cleaned. On his lunch break he cabbed over to Sim's. The woman behind the window where payments were handled remembered the car's interior cleaning. They did washes and only rarely had a request for car cleaning. She referred him to Carlos as the man who did the upholstery cleaning and paged him to the waiting area.

Carlos dropped out of the washing crew and came over to Bert.

"What can I do for you, Mister?" Carlos was friendly with a cautious manner.

"I'm the owner of a car you cleaned the other day, a red Toyota Camry."

"Why, is something wrong?"

"No, not at all. I just wanted to thank you for a very good cleaning job and give you a little something extra." He handed Carlos a folded twenty-dollar bill.

"Why is everyone so interested in that car? I left the gun alone, I never touched it. I even showed it to the woman who drove it in here. I didn't want anything to do with the gun."

"There's no trouble with the gun, Carlos. Did the woman say anything about it?"

"No, she hardly looked at it. I put the seat back in place and she took off."

"Did you get a good look at the gun?"

"Yeah. It looked new and had a telescope on it. I didn't get very close to it."

"That's fine, Carlos. One more thing. Can you describe the woman for me?"

"Nothing much to describe. Plain looking white woman about fifty."

Bert took out a picture from his wallet. It was one of Terry and him, taken shortly before their divorce. He handed the picture to Carlos.

"Is this the woman?"

"No. The woman with the car was not as pretty. She was plain. And her hair was very short. This is not the woman." He handed the picture back to Bert.

"Thanks, Carlos, you've been very helpful. Here's another twenty for your time."

Carlos looked hesitant. Bert could see he had something else he wanted to say.

"What is it, Carlos? Is there something else you want to tell me?"

"Yeah, there is. I don't know if it's important to you but another woman came by asking about the gun. I told her what I told you. That's it."

Bert was taken aback. Another woman. Could it have been Terry?

"Was it the woman in the picture I showed you?"

"No, no. This woman was some looker. Very pretty and younger than the woman who brought the car in. That's all I've got."

"Thanks again, Carlos. Hey, what time do you finish here in case I need to ask you to identify a woman in a picture?"

"Oh, six thirty, if I'm lucky. But later, if there are still cars to wash. It's a long day."

Bert left the carwash and went into a nearby Starbucks. He had to put this all together. A black coffee and a piece of lemon cake with icing would suffice for his lunch. He was due back in the office in half an hour.

Carlos was the connection between him and the sniper rifle. He was the only one who had actually seen the rifle and could possibly identify it. But there was no sniper rifle anymore. He had gotten rid of it. Seemed like the case against him was moot without the rifle. But if Carlos was questioned it could be trouble. And then there was the woman whom Carlos had told about the rifle. Who was she and why was she curious about the carwash incident? He pondered the situation.

If I eliminate Carlos this mystery woman can only offer secondhand information. With no gun and no Carlos I should be safe.

He finished his piece of cake and went outside to find a cab to get back to his office.

CHAPTER FIFTY-SIX

"This is WNYC's weekly TV magazine, *It's Happening Now*. Today the program is devoted to a single topic: the sniper. We have a panel of five people, each with a different interest in the subject. We'll hear from each of them and then allow the panelists to question fellow panel members. Then we'll have an open mike and take questions and hear opinions from listeners. It promises to be a lively hour. I'm Lowell Somers, the program's moderator. Okay panelists, let's get started with law enforcement represented by New York City senior homicide detective, Lieutenant Lionel Cobb."

Cobb explained the problem police were having identifying the sniper. He used his remaining three minutes to assure the public the police had abundant evidence from each crime scene, had added additional manpower to the sniper taskforce, and were committed to catching this murderer much as they would any killer.

Next, Trevor Bishop, Chief of Psychiatry at Stony Brook Medical School, gave a textbook description of a sniper with a well-defined target population. Max Gruen, president of the American Jewish Congress, spoke next.

"Jews were not conflicted. They side with the sniper in despising violent anti-Semitism, but abhor the murder of people whose only crime is speaking their minds about Jews."

He discussed the misunderstood pacifism of Jews in Europe during the Holocaust and contrasted it with the highly effective military force today in Israel.

Fourth to speak was Herman Midler, representing America for Americans, an organization known for its overt anti-Semitic rhetoric. Midler was quick to point out that innocent members of his organization were the targets of the sniper and that he himself felt threatened.

"None of the sniper's victims were guilty of any crime against Jews. They exercised their First Amendment rights and were murdered for that."

He questioned whether law enforcement was as committed to eliminating the sniper as they said. He asked why they'd had no success to date.

The panel grew restless as Midler spoke. Somers reminded them that they would have an opportunity to ask questions of each other after the last panelist spoke.

Leslie was the last panelist to speak.

"I represent the media. I'm also the only person who has actually spoken to the sniper. I spoke to him twice on the telephone and was able to authenticate his identity. You may have read my piece in *The Times* spelling out the sniper's position. It was verbatim what he told me over the phone.

"I have close contact with our homicide police, I've consulted several psychiatrists, and I've had the opportunity, with Mr. Midler's help, to meet a number of his colleagues. A fellow reporter at my paper met with Jewish leaders and discussed his meeting with me. I tell you this to assure readers that the media are doing their utmost to capture the full story for their readers. I for one have never been more caught up in a story than I am in this one."

Leslie could tell she had the panelists' rapt attention. She hoped the viewing audience was similarly engrossed and that the sniper was in that audience. She had a message for him.

"I don't know if the sniper is watching the show. If you are, I hope you'll call in and offer an opinion about what you've heard. You'll have to authenticate yourself if you do. Just repeat the information you used when you called me the second time."

Bert and Terry Alder were glued to the television set in her apartment. Bert was especially focused on Leslie.

"Didn't we meet that news lady at our hospital party some months ago?"

"Yes, we did. I know you took notice of her. Very prolonged notice, I might add. Funny thing, she had lunch with Diane and me the other day. She's a longtime friend of Diane. We had a good time. I guess I never told you about Diane's minor mishap with our car. She had to have the back seat cleaned and saw old Rosebud under the seat. You never told me you were storing it there. The three of us had a good laugh when we looked under the seat."

Bert was distracted from the television program. "Three of you? What three?"

Terry was surprised at Bert's insistence. "The lunch trio, Bert. We heard Diane's story and came back here to check it out. That's all there is to it."

"So this news lady was there when you looked under the seat and saw Rosebud?"

"Yes, Bert. Can we just watch the program now?"

"I'm sorry, your story distracted me."

Bert was putting two and two together. This news lady on the program was undoubtedly the woman Carlos had spoken to about the gun. For some reason she had gone to the carwash after seeing Rosebud.

Somehow she wasn't satisfied with Diane's story and w anted to verify the gun finding with the carwash attendant. Nosy woman. Smart woman. The program was now in the stage where panelists were allowed to question each other. Midler was quick to go after the police and wonder why they were finding this particular killer so elusive.

"Is public opinion blunting the police investigation? Seems this killer has acquired a Robin Hood image in this Jewish city. He's just like that vengeful killer in the movie *Death Wish*."

Cobb was quick to respond, "That kind of innuendo is totally out of line, Midler. I sympathize with the threat the sniper poses to you and your colleagues, but to the police a killer is a killer and we want the city rid of him."

Trevor Bishop, the psychiatrist, pointed out that the sniper wasn't just some extreme political activist. He was a murderer and was a threat to more than just Midler's colleagues. Leslie noted that Gary's warning to her carried this same message.

The call-in phase of the program allowed carefully vetted callers to voice opinions. There was a lot of support in the viewing audience for the sniper's position but for the most part people were unwilling to support murder of innocents as an acceptable response to the recent atrocities.

One perceptive caller asked Midler what America for Americans was doing about the threat. Midler gave a veiled response, implying that his organization was now taking an active role in bringing the sniper to justice. When pressed on this point he refused to be more specific.

The program wound up without breaking any new ground compared to what had already been reported in the press. Failure of the sniper to call in was disappointing.

CHAPTER FIFTY-SEVEN

The tenement in Queens had the usual odors of cooked food and rotting waste. The air was musty from a lack of ventilation. Climbing the stairs to his fifth-floor walk-up was his equivalent of a gym workout. Carlos lived alone in a one-bedroom apartment. His wife had left with their two-year-old son nearly one year ago. He put down the bag with his groceries and six-pack of beer to fish his keys out of his pants pocket. He let himself in and put the groceries on the kitchen table. He was exhausted after a full day in the carwash and the climb up to his apartment left him drained. Carlos settled into the well-worn easy chair and was half asleep when the doorbell rang.

He shuffled to the door and opened it without asking any questions. An unfamiliar face greeted him. The man wore thick black-frame glasses and had a short beard and moustache. His Greek fisherman style cap covered his eyebrows. He was dressed in jeans and a pullover grey sweater. He barged in past Carlos and shut the door. That was when

Carlos saw the gun in his hand. Before he could say anything he was shot once in the face just above his left eye. He was dead when he hit the floor.

The silencer on the gun blunted the noise of the single shot. Bert had followed Carlos home from the carwash. He had no interest in anything in the apartment, so he left, closing the locked door behind him. He met no one going down the stairs and was out of the building in less than a minute.

The body was discovered two days later when the manager at the carwash called the police about a missing worker who didn't answer his phone. There were no clues to start an investigation. The homicide was lost in an article in *the Daily News*, briefly sketching out a multitude of crimes committed over the week in the city. *The Times* gave it no space.

CHAPTER FIFTY-EIGHT

Lionel Cobb met Leslie in the 57th Street diner. The mayor was putting a lot of heat on the police commissioner to see some progress in the sniper case. The TV program had unleashed criticism from the city's diverse constituencies. All groups felt the killings only made divisions in the community worse. They all wanted to see an end to the violence, even if they held differing views regarding the sniper's stated justification.

"I don't have any progress to report, Leslie. Since the Loftus shooting the sniper has held his fire."

"I have something, but I'm hesitant to lay it out. I'd like to walk you through it as I saw it and see what you make of it."

"Leslie, anything is better than nothing. Lead me to it."

"Okay Lionel, let's get in your car and drive over to the Eastside. Sim's Carwash is on 103rd Street off First Avenue."

They drove over to the carwash. Leslie offered little background so they rode. At the carwash Leslie looked for Carlos but he was nowhere to be seen. Checking at the pay window she learned that Carlos had not been at work for several days. The manager confirmed that Carlos had not come to work recently.

Leslie walked over to Cobb, sitting in the police car. She explained that the man she wanted him to speak to was not at work and hadn't been for several days. The manager told her he even left his pay envelope at work. This was very unlike Carlos.

Cobb perked up. "What was Carlos's last name, Leslie?"

"Don't know, Lionel. Let me ask the manager."

Leslie returned in a minute. "Montanya. Carlos Montanya. That's who we're looking for."

"I've got news for you, Leslie. Carlos Montanya was found murdered in his apartment two days ago. Now, why don't you fill me in on what you know? Seems like our trip over here has taken on new meaning."

Leslie told Lionel the whole story, including her suspicion that Bert Alder was the sniper. *Poor Carlos*, she thought. An innocent carwash guy gets in the way of a homicidal avenger.

"That's quite a story, Leslie. All triggered by some spilled soup in the back seat of a car. Of course, Carlos's murder may be totally disconnected from the sniper story. I don't believe that but we have to consider the possibility. So, what do we have? No rifle. A dead witness who said he saw a rifle in the car. Could have been a sniper rifle. An old pellet gun in its place under the back seat of the car. A nosy reporter who says the dead carwash guy told her he saw a rifle that could be a sniper gun. A very smart sniper who's bound to deny switching the guns if he's ever questioned. I don't think the D.A. is gonna buy it. He may want to but there's no hard evidence of anything."

"I don't disagree, Lionel, but I'm sure we've got our man."

Cobb was silent as he thought through his next move.

Leslie watched him and waited.

"If I put a twenty-four-hour tail on him and wait for the next trigger event to send him out hunting we might catch a sniper. Trouble is, with no convincing evidence he's the sniper he'd have a good case for harassment if he found out he was being watched. I'll be sticking my neck out, but I'll do it anyway. This is all we've got after eight unsolved murders. I'll get the commissioner to buy into it to give me some cover. He's feeling the heat. I bet he'll bite."

Twenty-four-hour surveillance began the next day with a select crew of four detectives. The men were given a very abridged briefing on the case and the reason for the surveillance. The surveillance plan was labeled "Top Secret" and only Cobb and the police commissioner were aware of the basis for the plan's existence.

CHAPTER FIFTY-NINE

The Metropolitan Opera was opening its season at Lincoln Center with a pre-opera gala in the lobby. Wall-to-wall New York celebrities were present, including noted art dealer Ernst Cummings. He circulated around, drink in hand, looking for a lucky lady who'd share his company after the opera. The mayor was deep in conversation with the police commissioner. Their two wives were left to wander on their own. Estelle McGuire, the commissioner's wife, was an old friend of Cummings. The two of them had served together on several art organizations. She intercepted him as he headed to the bar for a refill of his vodka on the rocks.

"Ernst, how are you? Haven't seen you at a party since the Philharmonic Annual. Is all going well with your gallery?"

"Absolutely, Estelle. And how is the wife of our commissioner? What scandalous rumors are running around in your pretty head?"

"Nothing that would interest you, Ernst."

"Estelle, your rumors are Grade-A material. You usually scoop even that dirt rag, *The National Enquirer*. What are you holding back?"

She paused and looked around as if someone might be eavesdropping.

"Oh, well, you can keep a secret. Especially one without any sexual implications." She waved her hand at him. "They have a sniper suspect under surveillance. That's all I know and you *definitely* didn't hear it from me."

"Interesting, Estelle, but that won't help me sell any expensive drawings or prints in my gallery."

"Didn't think it would, but I'm running low on gossip. That was the best I could do tonight."

The gentle gong indicated it was time to head into the concert hall.

"It was great seeing you, Estelle. Let's do lunch next week."

They separated and headed toward their very good orchestra seats. Ernst smiled to himself. At last he was beginning to see some daylight. He had a good connection on the police force. He hoped his friend might be able to get him some info on a member of that surveillance team. Ernst desperately needed to earn his fee. It was payable only on completion of his assignment.

A phone call the next day brought Timothy Bergeron into his gallery. Bergeron was a plainclothes detective who worked in the police department's office of internal affairs. After ten years as a hardcore detective he'd chosen to spend the rest of his years before retirement sitting at a desk. A close-call shooting had helped him make that decision. At forty, he was a rugged, red-headed, former college football star whose job and tough appearance belied his intelligence and sophistication. He and Ernst were good friends who shared an interest in theatre and the arts.

Ernst greeted him warmly and the two walked out to a local coffee shop. The late morning hour left a number of empty tables so they found a quiet spot in a corner.

"Hadn't heard from you for a while, Ernst. How's it going?"

"Nothing to complain about, Tim. The art market is holding its own."

"You must have something important on your mind, Ernst, to bring me down here. What do you need?"

Bergeron put on his best poker face, expecting a request from his friend that would require suspension of his sworn responsibility as a trusted officer of the law. This wouldn't be the first time.

"Okay, Tim. Here's what I'm after. I hear the police have placed a sniper suspect under top-secret surveillance. I just need the name of one of the officers on the surveillance team. That's all. Just a name."

"Jesus, Ernst! You're always sticking *my* neck out. I'll have to make some very discrete inquiries. I'll give it a try. That's all I can promise. Give me a week."

"I knew I could count on you, Tim. I owe you another night like the one we had last month with those two dancers from *West Side Story*."

"Yeah, that was bruising. Took me a week to recover but it was worth it. We can discuss our next double when I bring you the name you're after."

CHAPTER SIXTY

Gary could sense Leslie's frustration. They'd discussed her situation and he could only empathize with her. The knowledge she held was dynamite but she had to sit on it until the sniper proved her correct. Surveillance was the right step but there was no way to know how long it might take to bring down the sniper. If he chose to go into a dormant state, surveillance would be for naught. If he stayed down long enough, the police would grow frustrated and abandon the surveillance.

When Diane called Leslie about her trip to the carwash, she had to lie and tell Diane it didn't yield anything.

In the absence of any overt moves against the Jewish community, Bert Alder felt little compunction to go out and select a target. He and Terry had even planned a brief holiday in the Caribbean. Their lives were beginning to approximate their early years of marriage. They still maintained separate apartments and hadn't discussed trying marriage again.

Eating dinner with trays on their laps in front of the television set, they were stunned to learn of a kidnapping and killing of a Jewish family of five on vacation in the Poconos. It might have been hard to tell that it was a hate crime if the perpetrators hadn't painted swastikas on the naked bodies of the victims. Once again, Jewish leaders expressed their grief and outrage.

Bert and Terry sat in stony silence.

"What's the answer to this, Bert? There seems to be no way to curb this violence. The sniper hasn't made a difference. These hate people aren't under anyone's direction. I think these are manifestations of spontaneous hate. There's no solution in sight."

"You may be right, but the sniper is the *only* response that causes any pain in that community of hate. I think it's better than no response."

Terry slept over that night but she was going to visit her sister in Oregon for five days. Bert now owned a new rifle and checked it out to his satisfaction.

Lionel Cobb had his surveillance team on high alert following the latest atrocity. He expected a sniper hit within the week, based on past performance.

Timothy Bergeron delivered a single name to Ernst Cummings. Gerry Sloan was the officer's name. Ernst considered several approaches to identifying the suspect and settled on a simple plan: Don't contact the officer. Find out where he lives and shadow him on his next shift *without* telling him. Tim could get his home address and, ideally, when his next shift would take place. He put in a call to Tim Bergeron. After Ernst explained his plan, Tim reluctantly agreed to do his friend this additional favor.

The police wanted to catch the suspect in the act of preparing to do his sniping. Less ideal was to catch him *after* a shooting. Ernst, on the other hand, only wanted to identify him and carry out his assassination when it was safest to do the kill.

Armed with Gerry Sloan's address and his next scheduled shift, Ernst set out to tail Sloan from his home in Queens to begin his twelve-hour shift. They each traveled by car. Sloan drove to an area on the upper Westside. He parked on the street in a line of parking slots reserved for police. Cummings pulled into a parking garage less than a block away. When he came out of the garage he could see Sloan still sitting in his car. He wasn't sure if this was his surveillance post or if he was just passing some time until it was 6:00 p.m. The drive over from Queens had taken less time than Sloan expected so he'd arrived fifteen minutes early.

Ernst saw a convenient Starbucks from which he could keep an eye on Sloan. He ordered a coffee and took a seat at a counter facing out the storefront window. At 6:00 p.m. Sloan still sat in his car. He stayed there for the next half hour, suggesting that *this* was his surveillance look-out post. Ernst surveyed the buildings Sloan could monitor from his car. The street was lined on both sides by unglamorous three story brown-stones that also had below-street-level apartments with separate entrances to the street. Trash cans were stored in the below-street-level entry areas of most of the houses. This was not a high-end street, although you could never tell what the interiors of the houses looked like.

At a little after seven Sloan got out of his car and seemed to be watching a man who had emerged from one of the below-street-level apartments on the opposite side of the street. Ernst took note of which house he'd come out of. Sloan followed the man as he walked briskly east-ward. He turned down Amsterdam Avenue and entered a restaurant. Sloan found a vantage point across the street, another restaurant from which he could keep an eye on his prey.

Ernst decided this was a good time to head back to the house the man had come out of and see if his name was on a mailbox or doorbell. He assumed the man was going to have dinner. If he was just going to pick up a take-out dinner he might come back a lot sooner. It was a chance he was willing to take.

There was no mailbox, just a slot in the door for the mailman to slip in any mail. There was a doorbell, however, and a fresh appearing name-tag under the ringer. He thought it a recent addition since it was still very clean in spite of no protection from the elements. The name was

Alder. Just one name. Alder. He left the area, pleased with himself at how he'd gotten the name of the man he presumed to be the sniper.

He returned to his car and drove back to the garage near his apartment. His next step would be to plan the assassination of Mr. Alder. The presence of police surveillance complicated his plan. They played an unwitting role of protector for the suspect. Somehow he would have to get around their cover. The best plan he could come up with was to wait for the suspect to go to work in the morning and take his surveillance cop with him. He would then enter the apartment and wait for the suspect to return home. At that point it was a simple matter of surprise and murder.

The question was how to enter the apartment. The following day around noon, he searched all around the building, but could only see one entry door. Even in the rear there was no other entry. The windows were protected by bars, a not uncommon feature of ground level and lower apartments in New York City. The front door had to be his entry point, but it was a solid wood door with no glass panel to break that would allow him to reach in and release the lock. Trouble with working on the door's lock was his exposure to foot traffic a few feet above this below-street-level apartment. He concluded this plan wasn't going to work.

For the moment he was stymied. He decided to have an early dinner nearby and return before 6:00 p.m., assuming that was when Alder would return home from work.

After a quick dinner he returned to his Starbucks lookout post. Shortly after six Alder came home and let himself into his apartment. Ernst could spot the surveillance cop "passing the baton" to the night shift officer. He decided to watch and see if anything developed.

An hour later the suspect came out dressed in a dark outfit with a loose fitting jacket, a knitted cap, and a large, sagging backpack. He didn't seem to be heading for dinner. Ernst was sitting double parked in his car and followed the suspect at a distance, mindful that the surveillance cop was tailing him as well, just ahead of Ernst. Tailing a walking man in a car was no easy job in Manhattan where traffic lights, double-parked cars, and one-way streets complicated the effort. Fortunately, Alder got into a cab, making it much easier to follow him. The cab didn't go far. Alder got out, walked down a driveway to an aboveground parking area behind an apartment house. He emerged a few minutes later driving a car. The two men in pursuit stayed on his tail.

The trip took them into the northern Bronx. Alder gave no indication that he was aware of the tailing cars. He drove slowly through a business area and past a storefront where people, mostly men, were gathering. It was past eight o'clock and the temperature was approaching fifty-five degrees. He circled around the block and did another drive-by. The storefront crowd was beginning to move into the store and it was apparent that some kind of meeting or assembly was going to take place. Ernst could see some of the men wearing leather jackets with swastikas painted on the back. Red and Black banners indicative of the neo-Nazi cause could be seen through the storefront window.

A park across the street extended for several blocks along this neighborhood shopping avenue. The park was one or two stories above street level with a steep incline facing the street. A pedestrian path wound its way up and disappeared as it neared the top. The park was poorly lit and no people could be seen in it. On the far side of the park, roughly fifty to seventy yards away, the park sloped down gradually, ending in a parallel street. This street was residential on its far side.

Ernst imagined that the suspect had selected this park for viewing and shooting. He'd have a good view of the storefront and an easy escape route across the park away from the commercial street.

Sure enough, Alder parked his car on the residential street and headed into the park with his backpack. The surveillance cop quickly parked in an illegal space. He put his police business placard on his dashboard so it would be readily seen by any curious policeman. He quickly left the car and picked up the suspect's trail.

Ernst had to scramble quickly to find a parking space. The one he found was a long block away from where Alder had entered the park. He walked briskly, entered the park, and tried to find Alder or the cop following him. The park was more heavily wooded than it appeared from the street. Finding either man in the dark was going to be difficult.

Alder found a good vantage point for watching the storefront and made himself comfortable. Perry Calkin, his police tail, was trying to find him in the now very dark woods. There was no moon tonight. Lastly, Ernst Cummings was at a loss to identify either of the two men who entered the park ahead of him. The park was very still.

Using a small directional microphone and headphones, Alder was able to pick up much of the speechmaking from the storefront. It was not ranting, but rather clearly stated standard anti-Semitic hate speech. He paid it little attention except that he could see the speaker near the open doorway. The size of the crowd had necessitated the doorway be kept open. Alder sighted on the speaker and took him down with a single shot. He also took down a young "brown shirt" in the crowd wearing a swastika armband. He calmly packed up and headed back to his car.

The police tail had not witnessed the sniper in the act but had heard the two shots. He moved to a vantage point where he could see the mayhem down below across the street. Ernst Cummings saw the man looking at the scene below and in the dark mistook him for the sniper. He shot him twice in the back. Perry Calkin pitched forward and tumbled down the steep incline to the street. Scattering people saw the body on the sidewalk across from the storefront but steered clear of it.

Bert Alder heard the two shots and decided to accelerate his pace, leaving the park. He got to his car and left the scene, driving sensibly so as not to attract any attention. The rest of the evening was uneventful for him.

Ernst Cummings also left the park at a leisurely walking pace. He too wanted to attract no attention. He was satisfied that he'd completed his assignment and would be paid as soon as news of his success reached his paymaster.

The 6:00 a.m. surveillance officer waited in Manhattan for his past evening counterpart. When Calkin failed to show he just began his shift watching the apartment. He put in a call to his group leader, alerting him to Calkin's absence.

CHAPTER SIXTY-ONE

First responder police investigating the triple killing were puzzled by the body of a dead police officer across the street from the store where the speaker and a crowd member were shot. The officer was not in uniform. The other two casualties were seemingly the victims of a sniper. There were numerous witnesses to the sniper shooting, but no one could say where the shots were fired from. The dead policeman had wounds suggesting a different weapon was used to kill him.

When homicide police arrived, inspection of the dead officer revealed that his clothing was soiled with dirt and his jacket torn in a number of places. They concluded that he had been shot in the park above the street and had fallen from there. Not until word reached the surveillance team leader was it apparent that the dead officer had been killed while tailing their suspect. The possibility had to be considered that a third party had been operating in the park and shot the officer in error while the sniper was disengaging.

Leslie heard all this news from Lionel Cobb. Their push for a surveillance operation had claimed one officer's life and brought them no closer to closing down the sniper. The idea of a third person's involvement was intriguing. It suggested that some leak of information about the surveillance had taken place.

Leslie and Lionel put their heads together and tried to imagine a three-man scenario. Leslie pulled Gary into the thought session. It seemed straightforward that the policeman was tailing the suspect, leaving the third man two possible objectives. Killing the officer seemed a poor strategy. The enraged police would replace him. Killing the sniper was a more promising objective. But why? Who would benefit?

The city's political leaders would get some credit for ending the siege. Getting hard evidence that the suspect was the sniper was proving difficult, so just going outside the justice system and eliminating the sniper was not a bad option. But who would take responsibility for *this* assassin?

Gary broke his silence. "The assassin benefits the neo-Nazis. He ends the sniper's killing spree and lets them breathe easy. They're the logical sponsors of this third man. He's a hired assassin, hired by the neo-Nazis. But how did he identify the sniper? Somehow he got wind of the surveillance and let it lead him to the suspect."

"Good reasoning, Gary." Leslie was still uncertain about Gary's theory.

"So why does he kill the cop and let the sniper get away?"

Lionel offered an explanation. "Good question, Leslie. But there's a simple answer: mistaken identity. He thought he killed the sniper. It was dark and the officer was at the edge of the park looking down at the chaos below. He shoots him in the back, never getting a good look at his victim. The officer pitches forward, falling to the street below. There's no opportunity to confirm his victim's identity."

Leslie shook her head from side to side. "It's a good story, Lionel, but there's no way to prove any of it and it relies on a killer's mistake."

Cobb saw the leak of information about the surveillance as crucial.

"I plan to interrogate each officer involved in the surveillance. Maybe it'll turn up a lead on the third man."

Leslie was in a somber mood. "So once again the sniper strikes and walks away with clean hands. He even took the time to shoot a crowd member he identified as a neo-Nazi supporter. This was just dessert for him. He didn't even know if the guy was a serious player in the hate crowd. He just had an arm band."

CHAPTER SIXTY-TWO

The paved pedestrian lane along the Hudson River was a very private meeting place at night. Most people avoided the path for the very reason Ernst chose it. There was a sense of insecurity in the less well-lit areas, far from the bright lights and busy streets of the upper West Side that lay across the West Side Drive. He sat and waited uneasily for his two paymasters, but there would be no pay for him tonight.

The newspapers covering the shooting last night gave out the bad news. One dead cop and two dead neo-Nazi supporters. The sniper had done it again and walked away. Herman Midler and Erich Voight could be heard approaching. Ernst rose up from the bench and greeted them with tentative handshakes.

Midler was first to speak. "Very disappointing, Cummings. I'm assuming you were there and shot the policeman. That's not what you were hired to do so it's certainly not what we're prepared to pay for."

"I'm not expecting to get paid for a case of mistaken identity. The good news is that I know the identity of the sniper and won't make the same mistake again. Just be patient. You'll get the result you want."

Voight was silent. He had recommended Cummings and felt a bit guilty in light of his man's screw up.

Midler kept the heat on. "We're not here tonight to tell you we're cancelling our arrangement. We *are* telling you that the clock is running and we expect results before the end of the month. Can you deliver?"

"I can and I will. I'm as disappointed as you are. It makes me doubly determined to succeed."

"That's all we have to say, Cummings. Erich and I are of a like mind on this. You were chosen based on very strong references. Call us when the assignment is completed."

Ernst watched the two men disappear into the darkness.

Bert Alder read *The Times* in Terry's apartment while he drank his morning coffee and ate a toasted bagel. He was learning for the first time what those shots he heard as he left the park were all about. A policeman was probably killed in the park and had then fallen to the street below.

Why was a policeman in the park? And who shot him? This was most bothersome to Alder. He seemed to have escaped by chance, just missing those two other people. He could only assume he'd been followed by one or the other or both. In either event, the third man in the park was the danger. The policeman had been watching him and followed him to the park.

That means I'm on some suspect list, he thought. He was glad he'd ditched the gun before coming up to Terry's place. She was away for a few days so he'd just hang out there after work.

Surveillance of Bert Alder's apartment was proving useless. There was no evidence that he was even in the apartment. Calkin's death had interrupted the chain of information on the suspect's location. Still, the police chose to continue the watch.

CHAPTER SIXTY-THREE

L unch break at the pediatric clinic found Bert eating a sandwich at his desk. The past week had been extremely stressful. He knew some people had him under suspicion. And it wasn't just the police. Some other party was out there gunning for him. The park episode had been a bizarre affair. Some hired killer had probably mistaken the policeman for him. He and the killer may have been very close in the dark woods and passed each other like ships in the night, going in opposite directions. He didn't like the position he found himself in, the target of someone he didn't know.

Reflecting on recent events, Bert was experiencing feelings not unlike those he felt when he first embarked on the sniper path: a feeling of renewal. The difference was that the feelings were opposite in direction; a return toward his life as it existed before the sniper emerged. His renewed relationship with Terry was pulling him back into mainstream life. His mother may have unconsciously competed with her for his love and made it difficult for Terry to fully win him over.

Bert realized he was engaging in bootstrap psychology but it made sense to him. With his aged mother's health failing he had moved out of the mainstream. There had been no loving Terry at that time to keep him from moving into a vengeful mode. The hate he shared with his mother had taken over. Now, with Sophie gone, his renewed love for Terry and her newfound love for him were diminishing the influence of his hate. He wanted to resume a normal life with her and allow the sniper to recede far into the past. He marveled at how this change came over him. He didn't regret the past killings; he just saw them as the result of an unhinged period in his life that he was now struggling to bring under control.

He wondered if the mysterious third man would allow him to assume this new life.

CHAPTER SIXTY-FOUR

The basement conference room in central police headquarters was rarely used since the second floor conference room had been remodeled. It gave the meeting a wartime atmosphere. Its raw concrete walls and the absence of windows gave it the look of a bunker. That was fine with Lionel Cobb. He wanted the surveillance team to feel the serious nature of this meeting.

"You're all here on time so I'll get the meeting started. We all regret the death of Perry Calkin. A fine young man and a decorated officer, Perry died in the line of fire. His death came as a big surprise since we're in surveillance and don't expect to encounter hostile fire. I've expressed the department's deeply felt sorrow to Perry's mother and father.

"Now, to the purpose of this meeting. We believe the man who killed Perry was aware of our surveillance operation and followed him as he tracked our suspect.

This operation is labeled 'top secret' and that means no discussion with anyone outside of those of us in this room. I'm going to ask each of you individually if you're aware of any leak. Even an inadvertent leak may have proven fatal for Perry. I'm starting with you, Mark."

Cobb went around the room and encountered no evidence that the remaining three officers were aware of any leaks. He was satisfied. The four-man team had been assembled with care and each man took his appointment as a mark of the regard his seniors held him in. He thanked the men for their cooperation and indicated the surveillance would continue until further notice. A replacement for Perry Calkin would join the team tomorrow.

That evening, Lionel met with Leslie and Gary and told them there was no progress on finding where the leak had come from. Lionel appreciated Leslie's role in identifying the suspect. Cobb's close cooperation with a member of the press would have been frowned upon by his superiors, but he held Leslie in high regard, both for her ethical nature and high intelligence. Gary was now held in similar regard. Nevertheless, their meetings were always kept secret. Tonight, Leslie, Gary, and Cobb were focused on the source of the third man's information.

Cobb was deeply disturbed. "Someone outside the surveillance team gave this killer the clue he needed."

Gary was excited and blurted out, "That's it, Lionel. The third man didn't need the suspect's name. He only needed the name of one officer on the team."

"I'm not following you, Gary. How does that get him to the suspect? Oh, wait a minute. Now I get it. Get a single officer's name, get his address and follow him to his surveillance post. That gets you to the suspect's home area. When a man emerges and is followed by a team member, you have the suspect's address and can then back into his name. Very clever, Gary."

Leslie kept the momentum going. "The question, Lionel, is who leaked the team member's name to the killer? I have to rely on you here. Who knew the names of the members of this top-secret team? Going back one step, who even knew there was a team? Remember, it was all very hush-hush."

"Leslie, I knew and the police commissioner knew. Even the mayor was kept in the dark. You knew. Gary was only brought in after the park shooting. So, me, you, and Commissioner McGuire. I can vouch for myself and I see you shaking your head in agreement. That leaves the commissioner. How do you think we should proceed?"

"You take the commissioner, Lionel. Is he married?"

"He is, to a woman in her early fifties. Her name is Estelle McGuire. They've been married for fifteen years. I'm not placing her under suspicion but I think she deserves our attention. She's all yours, Leslie. Just step lightly. Very lightly."

"Lionel, I'm thinking the commissioner may not recall leaking any information or may be too embarrassed to admit it. So even a negative after your interview with him wouldn't be sufficient to stop our search. That's a page from this reporter's workbook."

CHAPTER SIXTY-FIVE

The office of the police commissioner was more modern than the exterior of the classic federal style building suggested. It was tasteful and more comfortable than the usual glass and steel furnishings. The wall hangings were mostly abstract but not distracting. All in all, Lionel found it curiously inviting.

"Come in, Lionel. You're expected."

The commissioner came out from behind his large steel desk in his shirtsleeves and warmly shook Lionel's hand. They were old friends, on a casual basis.

"Credit Estelle with the décor. She did it all. Cost a pretty piece of change but the city kicked in most of it. Anyway, it worked out well, don't you think?"

"Absolutely, Hank. She has an eye for interior design."

"I'll tell her you said so, Lionel. She likes to be stroked. Now, why are you here? I'm at your disposal for at least fifteen minutes."

"You know about the death of one of our surveillance officers. We think there may be a killer out there who's trying to eliminate the sniper. He may have killed Officer Calkin in a case of mistaken identity. That's all supposition but it holds up pretty well to examination. Question is, how did this killer find out the identity of our suspect? That's why I'm here.

"The only people supposed to be in the know about the surveillance are the four—now three—officers, me, and you. I've questioned the three men and can vouch for myself. None of us leaked any information. So that leaves you and indelicate me has to ask the question. Did you leak any information inadvertently to anyone? That information may simply be that there was a suspect under surveillance. No names. Just that bit of information."

"Relax, Lionel. I'm innocent and you're doing the right thing in asking."

"Since you're not in a head-chopping mode, Hank, let me ask one more question. Did you casually tell Estelle about the surveillance?"

"Now I *am* ordering my men to set up the guillotine. Only kidding, Lionel.

Again I have to plead innocent. If I did, I don't recall doing it. I know that's a nuanced innocent plea, but it's an honest one. Are we done? I hope so, because I have a lunch date five minutes ago with the head constable of the London Police."

"Of course, Hank. I'm out of here. Thanks for your time and the candid responses. Much appreciated."

Lionel called Leslie as soon as he was out of the office building.

"As anticipated, the commissioner had no recollection of any leak. He even denied any leak of information to his wife though he qualified that with a disclaimer, 'If I did, I can't recall doing it.' That leaves it in your hands, Leslie. Good luck with the wife."

CHAPTER SIXTY-SIX

"Yes, this is Estelle McGuire. What can I do for you, Ms. Nugent?"

Leslie heard a friendly voice and was going to try to keep it sounding friendly.

"I'm a reporter with *The New York Times*, Mrs. McGuire, but the reason I called is not newspaper business. I'm seeking information you may or may not have. It might be best if we did this face to face. I don't say this to alarm you in any way because the questions I want to ask aren't of an alarming nature."

Leslie paused and hoped she'd aroused the other party's curiosity.

"I may regret this, Ms. Nugent, but why don't we meet for coffee at The Dark Roast on the corner of Third Avenue and 63rd Street in half an hour? Can you make that?"

"I'll see you there. I'm wearing a dark green belted raincoat. My hair is long, straight, and dirty blond."

Twenty minutes later Leslie was sitting at a corner table in The Dark Roast. A woman came in, looked around, and her eyes settled on Leslie who waved to establish contact. The woman was dressed smartly in a short leather jacket and rust colored corduroy slacks. She was trim with short, straight black hair. She was an attractive fiftyish woman who took very good care of herself. She indicated to Leslie that she was going to pick up a coffee and would bring one over for her. Obviously the friendly voice over the phone was in character.

Estelle brought the coffees over and settled into the chair opposite Leslie.

"Okay, Ms. Nugent, dispel the mystery. What are you after?"

"Call me Leslie, Estelle." Without a pause Leslie continued, "I'm going to dive right in. The police have identified a sniper suspect and initiated a top-secret surveillance project. Very few people know about this. Your husband, not surprisingly, is one of the few. Now here's the question, were you aware of this police action before I just told you? Please take the time to consider your answer."

The woman opposite changed from a smiling face to a stony one. She stared straight ahead at Leslie. The reporter could hear the wheels grinding in Estelle's mind. Her answer was going to be a carefully considered response and not a simple no.

"I guess I had an inkling about it. My knowledge was very vague. Barely more than a hint."

"I appreciate your honesty, Estelle. Now comes the hard part. Did you tell anyone what you knew, even if the information was no more than a 'hint'?"

Again, the woman opposite paused and seemed to be searching her memory. Then it dawned on her that she'd told Ernst Cummings about the surveillance when they met at the Met Opera opening party at Lincoln Center. She hesitated a moment to consider if she should divulge this innocent transfer of information to a Manhattan art dealer. She could sense that the reporter had an agenda. The questions had a bigger meaning than Estelle could decipher. She relented and admitted to loose lips. "Yes,

I told a friend what little I knew. It was just loose talk at a party. There was no conversation follow-up. We moved right on to other subjects."

"Thanks again, Estelle. Now, one last question. Who did you tell?"

Estelle was eager to end this interview and leave. She felt a faint coating of perspiration on her back and under her arms.

"Ernst Cummings. He's a Manhattan gallery owner. We're old friends and were just making small talk. That's all I know, Leslie."

"Estelle, you've been very helpful. I hope you didn't find my questions unduly stressful. I tried to keep them simple and straightfor-ward. I do appreciate your honest answers."

"If that's all, Leslie, I'll move along."

"Estelle, I'd appreciate it if you'd keep this conversation private. Tell no one about it. There are good reasons for me asking that of you. Will you do that?"

"I will. You can trust me."

CHAPTER SIXTY-SEVEN

Meeting with John Livingstone, her editor, was usually the highlight of her day. Today Leslie needed a highlight. She was weighed down by knowledge about two killers, one she was certain of and the other she was about to investigate. She had two potentially hot leads but neither with any corroboration, leaving them out of bounds for her pen. She shared her anxiety with Livingstone in his crowded office, overrun with newspaper clippings, books, and printed copies of emails.

"That's where I'm at on the sniper story, John. In deep, up to my nostrils and unable to print my way out of the swamp."

"Never short of metaphors though, Leslie. My concern is that you're assuming the role of detective and private eye when you're just a news reporter. I understand the job has elements of those two other roles. It's not easy to draw the line. My first caution is to be careful. Killers don't like prying eyes and ears. I admire your courage but don't want to write your eulogy. Not just yet."

"I'm with you on that score, John. I think the sniper is safely tucked away. His story is waiting to be told and I own most of it. It's the other guy who needs better definition. I'm going to report back to Lionel Cobb, my friendly homicide lieutenant, and see if he can carry the ball and serve as my protective shield. Are you okay with this plan?"

"I am, Leslie. You seem to be on top of the story and it'll be a whopper when you tell it. I know you're impatient as the pieces pile up, but I'm holding the reins of a horse that wants to gallop when she needs to canter. Let Cobb carry his weight here. Stay safe."

"I know this won't assure you, John, but you should know that I carry a legal pistol in my purse. I got it approved in Washington for self-defense based on my need to work in dangerous places and consort with less than savory characters. I'm actually a pretty good shot even though I've never had to use it to defend myself."

"That only makes me more nervous, Leslie, not less. Don't let the gun tempt you to take chances that mere mortals would avoid. I mean it, Leslie."

Cobb was her next stop. For this meeting she asked Gary to come along. She welcomed his insights and his ability to keep her grounded when necessary.

They met in Cobb's office behind a closed door. Leslie related the details of her conversation with Estelle McGuire.

Cobb was first to speak, directing his words to Gary. "This is what Leslie and I suspected would happen. The commissioner had no recollection of leaking the information to anyone but left the door open that an inadvertent slip was a possibility. I'm taking his words at face value. I know him and don't think he's protecting his wife. That's moot since she fessed up to Leslie and even named the person whom she passed it on to. Without even asking, Leslie, I assume you've already been online about this guy."

"I couldn't sit still, Lionel. The guy is Ernst Cummings, a reputable gallery owner in lower Manhattan. He's native born, about forty-four years old and divorced. He lives in Trump Tower and is well known in society circles. I asked around very discretely and learned that he's a serious lady's man. I didn't hear any connection to Estelle McGuire. Two items of interest came up. He's a high flyer and could be living above his means. His gallery is successful but business isn't anything to brag about. You might wonder how his income and expenses match up. I can't say, but he doesn't seem to have any other source of income anyone knows about. Second thing, his apartment house doorman says he frequently has good-looking women visiting his apartment. That's all I have. There's no criminal record."

"Gary, any thoughts?" Cobb wanted another mind working in the skull session. He knew and respected Gary.

"Could be the partial profile of a hedonistic guy who likes the good life. There's not enough here to go on. Big question is whether he has connections on the police force from whom he can pluck favors. He can't ante up big bucks, but maybe he can offer something else, like sexual opportunities, to cops who live in a low budget world. I'm just reaching here but somehow he must have access to top-secret police information to use that tip from Estelle to any advantage."

Cobb followed up on Gary's scenario. "That's good thinking, Gary. He knows there's a surveillance operation and won't learn anything from the team. All he needs is the name of one team member. He's not asking for a big favor but he can leverage it to find out what he needs to know. Clever. He follows that officer on his surveillance and identifies the suspect. This guy is no amateur."

Leslie was more than curious. "So, Lionel, who would *you* go to for the name of a top-secret team member?"

"I'd go to the commissioner's classified files. These files are governed by very restricted release criteria. They're guarded by security conscious police assistants."

Gary was keeping on this track. "So, a contact with access to those files might be able to get a name for him, if the contact was willing to violate the security of the files. How do we find out if Cummings has such a contact?"

Leslie offered a suggestion. "What if we show a photo array of officers with access to the commissioner's files to the doorman at Cummings's apartment building? It's a reach, but we're not getting very close by any other means. Say he picks one out as an occasional visitor to Cummings's apartment. Would that get us anywhere? I think that would begin to establish a chain of evidence linking Cummings to the suspect and possibly the shooting of Officer Calkin."

Cobb was working a different aspect of the case. "Okay, this speculation is worthwhile and I think it generated a direction to pursue. I like the photo array idea. I'm still wondering who Cummings is working for. I know that assuming Cummings is the guy is jumping ahead of the evidence. Nevertheless, since it's money he needs, some deep pocket must be sponsoring him. Question is why? The answer to that will tell us who. Gary, you had a good answer to this one several days ago. The 'why' is because the sniper is causing someone pain. That has to be the neo-Nazis. They're the likely paymasters. It gives us another avenue to pursue: find a connection between Cummings and some group, like America for Americans."

Leslie saw the need to wind up the session and move on the leads they'd identified. "Lionel, it looks like you're the guy to put together the photo array. Gary and I aren't in any position to assemble one. If that serves us up a leak in the commissioner's office we'll be off and running. In the meantime, Gary and I will take a shot at Midler and see if he has any connection to Cummings."

CHAPTER SIXTY-EIGHT

Bert and Terry were enjoying a quiet evening in their old apartment, which had become Terry's home after the divorce was sorted out. They each marveled at how they'd come back together, even more strongly than ever before. Terry attributed this stunning reversal in their feelings to a reinvented Bert. He was no longer the reclusive guy devoid of romantic feelings for her. His mood had changed dramatically and won her over completely. She accepted the change and had no intention of delving too deeply into the forces that had engineered it.

Along with the new feelings they felt had come a revitalized sex life. The sex was intense and passionate. Tonight they were playfully pawing each other on the living room sofa. "Playful" became heated and Terry's workout pants soon lay on top of Bert's on the floor. It didn't take long before they each reached a rousing climax.

THE SNIPER

Lying entwined on the sofa, Bert broached the subject they were each ready to entertain, trying marriage once again. Terry didn't hesitate. She voiced enthusiastic support for the idea.

Bert was in a quandary. He harbored a potentially destructive secret, but didn't want to destroy their newfound relationship by confessing to Terry. Going forward with a dark secret in his closet might eat away at him. He rationalized the sniper as past history that could be left to recede, with time, into the very distant past. He believed people learned to live with their secrets, even one as violent as his. At this time there was no evidence linking him to the sniper. He decided to move forward, carrying his baggage with him. He'd keep Terry in the dark. Forever.

CHAPTER SIXTY-NINE

S eafood paella was Gary's favorite dish and Leslie was striving might-ily to follow the recipe in *The New York Times Cookbook*. She'd tried it before with modest success but now, with that experience behind her, she'd bought *all* the right ingredients this time and was putting the finishing touches on her "masterpiece." *Great moments in courtship,* she thought.

They were relaxing with drinks in her apartment while the paella magic was staying warm in the oven. Gary could sense Leslie's distant mood. He tried to bring her out of it.

"Okay, Les, let me in. Whatever is haunting you would be better dealt with out in the open. Remember me? The reporter's best friend? I might be able to help."

"Gary, answer this question for me. If the sniper decided to 'stand down' could this be a *real* change? And by that I mean a permanent, substantive change in the man. After all the killing could he return to normal life?"

"I see. So the sniper is preying on you. Let me give it a try. Take addiction. I wrote a lot about this when I was in Los Angeles. The victim, alcohol or drug addicted, goes through a period of withdrawal and comes out of it, with help, as a clean human. The addiction potential is still there, but having beaten it, albeit temporarily, with a supportive environment and caring people, it can be a lasting state.

"The sniper is different. His addiction is to vengeance in reaction to certain violence. He can get 'clean' like those other addicts. Big difference is that the drug and alcohol addicts just have to say 'no' to drugs and drink. Then the addicting substance doesn't get into their system to work on them. They're in control. The sniper, though, is exposed to repeated instances of anti-Semitic killing. That's his drug or alcohol. He's *not* in control of that. It's not the same as turning down a drink or a fix. The killings do enter his mind, even against his will. They're also in his memory. He'd have to move to Pago Pago to be free of new violent actions that might set off his need for vengeance.

"Return to normal living? Superficially, yes. The question is, for how long? How will he react to the next violent act? Here we get to the crucial question. Just as there was a trigger in his life that set him off on the sniper course, there could be a life change or changes that offset that trigger. Don't forget, the sniper is a serial killer. And that propensity will always be there. If circumstances are favorable, though, he may never kill again. Just remember, a 'cure' is not the same as 'remission.'"

"Are you just spinning this theory out of thin air, Gary, or is this serious, mainstream addiction theory? I mean the part about the sniper."

"Leslie, the sniper is a work in progress. I don't think there's anything mainstream about him. Ideally he'd accept the help of a specially qualified psychiatrist or therapist. Unfortunately, the state law requires any caregiver to report the name of a murderer, past or potential, to the authorities. I doubt the sniper would be willing to put himself in that position."

"Maybe there's some way around that, Gary. We have to look into it."

Gary had more to say.

"Leslie, there is one other thing on my mind that we haven't touched on. Your sympathy for the sniper seems to be motivating you to spin his story in a favorable light. Especially when it comes to any possible chance for rehabilitation. What am I missing here? What's behind your support for this serial killer? Will it keep you from reporting the story objectively?"

"I can't say I disagree with your take on my sympathies, Gary. It's been difficult for me to stay neutral. You're asking why. I don't have a good answer but you've caught me stepping out of my journalist's requisite neutrality. Let me offer a few scraps of information. I'm not Jewish. You know this. There are no traces of Jewish blood in my background. My family roots are pure English, Irish, and Dutch.

"I grew up in a very waspish home free of any racial or religious prejudice. I had Jewish girlfriends and dated Jewish guys in high school and college. I think those contacts made me aware of certain qualities in Jews that I saw missing in my own background. I became partial to Jewish guys and had a few serious romantic affairs. I read a lot about the Holocaust, Israel's history, and anti-Semitism here and abroad. I think I became quasi-Jewish, absent any religious overtones. The sniper story grabbed hold of me. It was clear where my sympathies lay. I can't deny my tilt but I think it only carried me slightly off course. I'm aware of my feelings, not ruled by them.

"As the story developed I saw it clearly as a conflict between Jews and neo-Nazis. To some extent I bought into the sniper's justification. I sided with the Jews. To side with the neo-Nazis was to accept the Jews in an impotent condition, having to suffer the atrocities while the police offered no justice.

"I can see that my neutrality was challenged. Maybe it's asking too much of a reporter to always be neutral. Maybe I should be working on the opinion page of the paper. This story has forced me to rethink my relationship to charged news stories. But, maybe with maturity a reporter can do a better job if she invests some emotion in the issues. And with emotion some degree of neutrality may be lost."

She paused. "Does that offer an insight in answer to your question, Gary?"

CHAPTER SEVENTY

Assembling a photo array of the officers with access to the commissioner's top-secret files was not difficult. The challenge for Cobb was to keep his activity secret. If there *was* a "leaker" in the commissioner's office he needed to be unaware that his photo was being used to identify him as a contact with a suspected police killer.

Lionel Cobb had taken personal responsibility to carry out this task. It had only taken a few evenings of his time and the array was now ready to be shown to the doorman at Cummings's building. The array contained six pictures of detectives.

The Trump Tower doorman, Tom Gardner, was dressed in a black suit, white shirt, and striped tie, as were the other staff in the lobby. He'd been working in this building since it opened three years ago. Cobb hesitated to show his badge in full view of the staff. He motioned to Gardner to step outside with him. Once away from the others, Cobb showed the doorman his badge. He explained the reason for this visit and showed

Gardner the photo array. He disguised the photos in an unfolded subway map and told the doorman to tell the others that the stranger had asked for directions to the Whitney Museum in Chelsea.

Cobb held the map with the photo array while Gardner carefully studied the pictures. Without any hesitation he identified one person in the array. He said that the man in the picture was an occasional visitor for Mr. Cummings. Maybe once a month. He usually came in the early evening. Gardner never saw him leave, possibly because his shift ended at 8:30 p.m.

Cobb saw no need to question the others. He cautioned the doorman not to say a word to *anyone*, including Cummings, about this visit. He emphasized the point and asked if he had a problem with that. The doorman nodded that he didn't.

Cobb folded up the map, thanked him, cautiously slipped two ten-dollar bills into his suit jacket pocket and left.

He flagged a cab and headed downtown to his office. He marveled that sometimes things did go right.

The next step would be to interrogate the identified officer. Timothy Bergeron was a veteran detective and would be threatened by the questions. He had the option of asking for a representative of the police union to be present. Cobb was prepared for this and was willing to bargain with Bergeron. There'd be no formal interrogation. No record would be kept and nothing would be entered in his file. Cobb wanted an answer to two questions: Do you know Ernst Cummings and did you give him the name of a member of the surveillance team?

Again, the strategy worked. Bergeron met Cobb in a bar far from headquarters. Over beers, Cobb explained the terms of the question and answer session. Bergeron knew he'd been fingered. He felt Cobb's deal was as good as he could do. He knew about Calkin's death and he wondered if his simple action of giving Cummings Gerry Sloan's name in any way implicated him.

He answered Cobb's questions without trying to spin his answers. "Yes, I know Ernst Cummings and yes, I gave him Gerry Sloan's name."

He felt a need to add that Cummings never told him why he wanted a name.

Cobb realized that giving the name of any member of the team would suffice for Cummings to ID the sniper suspect. Even though Bergeron hadn't given Calkin's name to Cummings, Sloan's name gave Cummings what he needed. Calkin had paid the price.

Before they parted, Cobb warned Bergeron not to breathe a word about this conversation to anyone.

"You made a terrible mistake, Timothy. It may have caused the death of an innocent officer. You'll have to live with that all your life."

Cobb got up and left the bar. Bergeron sat there staring into his beer.

CHAPTER SEVENTY-ONE

The phone call from Lionel Cobb confirmed what Leslie had learned from Estelle McGuire. The pieces fell nicely into place. There *was* an assassin hired to eliminate the sniper. The assassin's identity was known. He also was very likely Officer Calkin's killer. The only hard evidence Cobb had was Bergeron's confession that he had given Cummings the name of an officer on the surveillance team. The rest of the story was pure conjecture, but added up to Cummings knowing the sniper's identity and following him to the park where Calkin was killed. Cobb knew the case against Cummings was very thin. The best he could do at this time was put him on surveillance on the chance that he would make another attempt on the sniper's life. It wasn't much but it was the best he could do absent any hard evidence.

Leslie sat in her office early in the evening considering her alternatives. She had carefully assembled the components a major story. All that remained was to decide how to handle the sniper's identity. There was no proof that Alder was the sniper but she *knew* he was. If he would confess to her off the record she might be able to go ahead with the story. She needed his confirmation of a number of facts. Writing the story without the sniper's name was a limitation. The confirmations she was seeking would surely indicate that she either knew his identity or at least had communicated in some manner with him. The story's credibility depended on convincing readers that she had gotten her facts from the sniper. She might be able to finesse his name.

Her discussion with Gary had given her an angle she needed to see if Alder was willing to stand down. There was no "cure" for him, only the possibility of "remission." Confessing to her had no standing in law and, besides, she was pledging to maintain confidentiality.

The case of the other shooter would be handled by Cobb and the homicide police. Any role for her in that matter would take second place to getting the primary story into print. Her next step would be a meeting with Bert Alder.

Leslie called Bert at his clinic that afternoon. When she identified herself he recalled briefly meeting her many months ago at a hospital party. Leslie told him she had a matter of utmost importance to discuss with him. She declined to offer any specifics but made it sound rather urgent. He had no doubt that it was about the sniper. He wanted to know how much she knew. He agreed to meet and offered his clinic office after hours as a neutral site where they'd have privacy.

They now sat face to face in his small office. The clinic had long since emptied of patients and Bert was the last remaining physician. He recalled the hospital gala and how he had trouble taking his eyes off her. He and Terry had been moving toward divorce at that time. He was a different guy now.

Leslie began the conversation by explaining why she wanted to meet with him.

"I'm going to call you Bert, if you don't mind."

"Go ahead, Leslie, I have a feeling this isn't going to be a very formal meeting."

"Good. Let's be as informal as possible. Bert, I'm trying to wrap up my story about the sniper and get it into print. There are a few clarifications I need and you're the only person I can think of to ask. I'm not wearing a wire and I've turned my phone off. I promise that this entire conversation will be off the record. I have no intention or desire to deceive you."

"Don't worry, I'm on guard and can protect myself. Get started."

Leslie paused briefly before beginning. She was more than a little unsure of herself. She desperately wanted to wrap up the story but also wondered if he could be saved. Or *should* be saved.

Leslie dove right in. "I know you're the sniper, Bert. Don't ask me how I know. I have knowledge that convinced me. It's hearsay but it fits too well to be anything but true. Now I'm here seeking answers to questions that trouble me. First, did you kill Carlos, the carwash attendant, to protect your identity?"

"You'll hear no confessions from me, Leslie."

"That's one of the sniper's killings that I find most difficult to justify. It was cold-blooded self-protection."

"Isn't self-protection justified in a time of war to continue waging the war? You can't tease apart each act done in the cause for justified vengeance and require a detailed rationalization."

Leslie took that as a yes and went on. "A young man wearing an armband was killed in the shooting across from the park several weeks ago. Again, this killing wasn't based on the young man having an outspoken role in the neo-Nazi cause. He was a sympathetic bystander and the sniper took him out just because he was there and wore an armband. This was not a carefully planned hit the way the speaker's killing was. Any comment?"

"Again, Leslie, in a time of war killing cannot be precisely controlled. How many innocents have we killed in Afghanistan? Vietnam? What about Dresden, Hiroshima, Nagasaki, Wounded Knee, My Lai and on and on?"

Leslie took his answer as an explanation, and an indirect confession.

"Okay, Bert, tell me what you think drove the sniper to abruptly turn into a violent avenger."

The conversation had veered into a third person discussion.

"We published his response to our letter in *The Times* but it didn't seem to be an adequate explanation. Ideologically it was rational, but why begin sniping at that particular time? Atrocities inflicted upon Jews in America weren't anything new."

Bert offered an answer in the same third person, but it clearly had a ring of personal insight. "The sniper may have been challenged at a vulnerable moment in his life. Imagine a man whose beloved mother was a Holocaust survivor. He was deeply troubled through all his life, beginning in childhood, by her frequent retelling of her family's suffering at the hands of the Nazis. This was his family. Perhaps the sniping was triggered by her approaching death. This may have taken place on the backdrop of a failing marriage. What I'm saying is there may be a *confluence* of painful life factors that drive a person to do things he normally would keep under control."

Leslie credited Bert with plausible insight. Surely he was talking about himself.

"That helps, Bert. Let's look ahead. Do you think the sniper can see the influence of those 'painful life factors' being muted? And if so, could the sniper then return to mainstream living?"

"Leslie, I can see the sniper establishing a loving relationship with a woman. I can also imagine him bringing the pain he shared with his now-deceased mother under control. Possibly, the sniping allowed him to imagine his mother's pain eased before her death. If these life factors took hold he might very well end his sniping. Forever? I would hope so. But that remains to be seen. Being 'cured' is not the same as 'going into remission.'"

Leslie was struck by the same analogy that Gary had used. She now believed the best that could be achieved for Bert was remission. With his history of killing, society would not accept that. It lacked finality and an appropriate punishment.

"Leslie, I have something to add. I've given a lot of thought to the sniper and I've reflected on his actions. Cold-blooded killers and especially serial killers rarely if ever show any remorse. I believe the sniper may have begun feeling remorse as his life improved and he initiated an attempt at turnaround. Carlos and the young man with the armband were two regrettable deaths. But so were the other victims."

He paused as he formulated the sniper's reflection on many months of planned assassination. Leslie was surprised by this statement of remorse. And encouraged. He went on.

"It's an enormous step for the sniper to concede that his victims were people who may have had lives filled with disturbing events much as he did. They were imperfect much as he was. Adopting the neo-Nazi ideology set them apart. Espousing that hateful dogma probably had roots in their life factors, some even beyond their recall. They were victims long before the sniper came along. Their families were badly injured by their violent deaths. Feeling remorse now for these tragedies is all he can offer. It may be a step back toward ordinary life for the sniper."

Leslie could feel the emotion behind Bert's words.

"Bert, if the sniper is truly coming to this realization there may be hope for him. The test will be if there is a cessation of the killings, and I don't mean for a few weeks. He has to stand down and mean it."

Leslie stopped here and the two of them sat in silence, pondering the implication of the words each had spoken.

"I think I have what I need to finish my story. I appreciate your honesty."

Leslie left the office with her head full of ideas to incorporate in the article.

CHAPTER SEVENTY-TWO

Ernst Cummings was determined to complete his assignment and collect his fee. He knew his target and thought he knew where he lived. To his surprise, when he went by the suspect's apartment the police surveillance was no longer in place. He had no idea why it had been called off. He knew the suspect was the sniper. After all, he'd followed him to the park, the scene of the most recent shooting. He didn't know that the surveillance team had reported the suspect must be living elsewhere. They no longer saw him enter and leave his apartment and therefore couldn't follow him anywhere. That was sufficient reason to call off the surveillance at the original address.

An increasingly anxious Ernst Cummings decided the next best place to end his interminable assignment was the suspect's place of work. While Leslie waited for the elevator on the fifth floor after leaving Bert's office, Cummings stayed hidden in the stairwell. When she left in the elevator he headed into the clinic area and began searching for Alder's office. All the doctors' offices were empty.

Bert came out of the men's room to find a stranger roaming around in the doctors' office area. He called out to the man who promptly spun around with a gun in his hand. Cummings only knew what Bert looked like from a staff photo array he saw in the vestibule to the clinic, so he hesitated momentarily before shooting. Once he thought he had his man, he got off two shots but his target was already in motion. His first shot missed and the second just inflicted a grazing wound on his left leg. Bert raced into the hall and headed down the stairs with Cummings in pursuit.

Leslie was almost out on the street when she heard the shots. She ran back in but had no idea where in the building the shots had been fired. She instinctively took her small caliber handgun out of her purse and went looking for Bert Alder. She knew that Bert was the target of an assassin who may have decided this was a good place to find and terminate his prey.

She heard two more shots up above and could hear running footsteps in the nearby stairwell. She cautiously ascended the stairs and suddenly encountered Bert coming down. His left pant leg was bloodstained. Another person was in hot pursuit and was only one floor above them. Bert tried to have Leslie join him in flight but she was thinking, *stand and fight.*

As the pursuer turned the corner, gun in hand, he came face to face with two people instead of one, and made his second hesitation error. Leslie didn't hesitate. She fired rapidly, twice at close range, and took down the shooter. Her first shot hit him in the shoulder and caused him to drop his gun. The second shot was dead center in the middle of his chest. He fell hard on the stairwell landing and didn't move.

Bert hugged Leslie. She was trembling from the near-death experience.

"My god, Leslie. That was something. I'm amazed how you stood your ground with that small pistol. You saved both our lives from this maniac's attack." Bert kept shaking his head and repeating, "Amazing. Just amazing."

Leslie got herself back under control.

"This guy seemed to want you dead in a bad way, Bert."

She cautiously approached the still form on the landing and pulled a wallet from his vest pocket. His ID told her all she needed to know. Another piece fit perfectly in the puzzle.

The police were clambering up the stairs and took over the crime scene. Bert and Leslie were held aside for questioning. They took her gun away along with the dead man's wallet. Bert's leg wound was treated by an EMT and declared non-threatening. The blood made it look worse than it was.

The entrance to the clinic building was cordoned off and the police were keeping everyone, including the press, outside that perimeter. Leslie and Bert regained their composure after the harrowing event in the stairwell. She sat sideways on the back seat of a police cruiser with the door open and her legs resting on the curb. Bert stood nearby. A policeman had them under his watchful eye. They were yet to be questioned by the police.

Leslie asked that Lieutenant Lionel Cobb be called to the scene. When an officer told her he was going to take her statement, she indicated that she preferred to give her statement to Cobb and that there were good reasons for that. Bert gave the same reason for withholding his statement. The officer backed off when Cobb's name was brought into the picture.

"Bert, let me do the talking when Cobb gets here. You can hear what I tell him, but wait until you hear it all before you give any statement to the police. Just listen."

Bert nodded his assent. He was extremely anxious with all the police attention he and Leslie had drawn.

"You just saved my life, Leslie! I think I'll go along with whatever you ask."

Cobb arrived and, after a brief recap from the officer in charge of the crime scene, headed over to Leslie and Bert.

"How are you two? I gather there were shots fired but you both look none the worse for close-up combat." He smiled and his effort to comfort the two survivors of the shooting had a soothing effect.

"We're both okay, Lionel. Maybe a bit shaken but that's beginning to wear off. Before we give our statement to the officer in charge, Lionel, I need a private moment with just you and Bert. Maybe we can do that right here in this cruiser."

"Sure, Leslie, that's fine with me." Cobb turned to Bert. "You must be Bert Alder. We've never met. I'm Lionel Cobb, the new Chief of Homicide for the city of New York." The two men eyed each other warily. Cobb didn't offer to shake hands.

Bert got into the cruiser next to Leslie and Cobb seated himself in the front passenger seat and turned to face them.

"Okay, Leslie, it's your show."

"Be patient with me, Lionel, as I spell out my idea."

Leslie paused and fought to maintain her composure. The impact of the events in the stairwell was still very much with her.

"Okay. We know someone hired Cummings to kill the sniper. If this evening's event is spelled out in clearest detail, Cummings may be perceived by his employers as having identified the sniper. I'm assuming he hasn't already passed along that information. His failed attempt to kill Bert will be interpreted by them as identifying the sniper. This would set Bert up for another assassination attempt.

"Bert, Lionel and I know all about your activities. But we have no hard evidence to back up what we believe to be the case.

"Now here's the tricky part. Lionel, we need to conceal Bert's identity and make him out to be an incidental person fleeing from a deranged shooter. If you can control the police report, Lionel, maybe you can conceal Bert's identity so that he's not seen as Cummings's intended target."

Cobb turned and looked Bert squarely in the eye. "Are you in full agreement, Alder? Leslie and I don't want this to come back and bite us. I'll have more to say after Leslie finishes."

"I think I understand what you two are trying to do, save my life. I can go along with that. Just help me stay on script so Leslie and I are on the same page."

Lionel opened the car door and got out. He approached the officer in charge and took him aside, "Officer Gentry, you have this scene well in hand. I've taken statements from the two people in the cruiser and will place their statements in the case file.

"The woman shot the assailant in self-defense, a rather gutsy, heroic stand on her part. The man was just fleeing the scene and was being chased by the assailant. He plays no important role in the attack by the dead man. I have their IDs and think it's safe to let them go. I have my reasons for taking an active role here. I hope you'll afford me some latitude and keep my involvement something between just the two of us."

"I understand, Chief. I know how to keep a confidence."

Cobb walked over to the cruiser and told Leslie and Bert what he did. He couldn't get over the reporter's courage.

"I never doubted you had it in you, Leslie, but until it's actually demonstrated, courage is something you can only wonder about."

Cobb was willing to go along with their immediate plan but his police instinct was flashing an amber light, not a green.

He pulled Leslie aside and offered the option he was considering once this shooting was wrapped up.

"Leslie, hear me out. My instincts tell me that we need to present something to Alder that's compatible with police ethics in handling a suspected serial killer. Hear me out.

"We follow your protective plan where Alder's identity is concealed in the story covering this shooting. The police place him under surveillance, as in the past. I will insist he wear a tracking bracelet. As a free citizen he could object to this but he's making a trade with us for concealing his identity.

"So, he either takes his chances as a free man with you reporting the shooting truthfully with Bert Alder as the gunman's target or you obfuscate his identity and he submits to constant surveillance. I suspect he'll opt for scenario two. Absent proof of the sniper's identity I can live with this should he elect the bracelet option."

Cobb and Leslie returned to Bert. Cobb presented the options to Alder. Leslie had agreed to maintain her silence during the deliberations.

"I know we're working on a tight schedule, Alder, but that's the hand we've been dealt. Leslie's original idea that we just conceal your identity doesn't fly with me. I insist on the addition of surveillance. I can only go so far on your behalf. I need your answer. Now."

Bert could see his options were severely limited. He opted for the bracelet.

CHAPTER SEVENTY-THREE

Even with a few loose ends, the final sniper story was ready to be written. The neo-Nazis who'd hired a killer would not be identified. There was no supporting evidence. Cummings, the clinic shooter, was a man on an undisclosed mission and he'd failed to carry it out. Suspicion was that the shooter had it in for someone in the clinic and chanced upon a pediatrician who was late leaving his office. The woman's reason for being in the clinic was described as personal. She was a friend of the pediatrician's ex-wife. She was meeting him for dinner to help foster the new relationship developing between the doctor and his ex-wife.

There was no evidence that Bert was anything other than a respected pediatrician. Leslie had decided that she'd tell the final story without implicating him. There was a far better story to be told if the sniper could be outed, but that option was not on the table. There still was no proof.

Tonight Leslie was meeting Lionel Cobb at his request. For both, this would be an opportunity to put the finishing touches on an unfinished story.

They met in a neighborhood restaurant near Chelsea in the late evening when the crowd had dissipated. Cobb wanted to bring Leslie up to date on the sniper case. He felt an unusual camaraderie with the reporter. In forty years on the force he'd never been close to any member of the press.

"As you know, Alder opted for the bracelet, Leslie. He knows that if he returns to action as the sniper I'll go after him seeking my own kind of vengeance. On the other hand, if the sniper stands down for good, I'll rest my case but just stay vigilant."

"I know this hasn't been easy for you, Lionel. I'm impressed with your ability to 'play against type,' as they say in Hollywood."

"I'm committed to surveillance for the life of the sniper. The bracelet has been put into effect without any fanfare. If I retire with the sniper still living, my successor as Chief of Homicide will be brought into my confidence and fully informed about what had transpired. The commissioner is privy to the step I've undertaken and swore there would be no leak from him. He understands that the information he innocently passed on to his wife about the earlier surveillance had cost an officer his life."

"You're a stand-up guy, Lionel. Alder is lucky he ran into *you* as Chief of Homicide. On a different note, I realize that Bert can't meet with a psychiatrist. Once he reveals his incredible past the psychiatrist is ethically and legally bound to turn him in. I think he realizes that. I believe you're doing the right thing, Lionel. This is a good way to wind up a bizarre story. I have one remaining concern, Lionel."

"Let's hear it, Leslie. I have a hunch it's the same one I'm harboring."

"The people who hired Cummings may see through the story and realize that he was onto the sniper. Bert's identity as the sniper may not be concealed in my story."

"Exactly, Leslie. He's a marked man. Now it remains to be seen if a second killer is hired to finish the job Cummings failed to complete. I won't offer a prediction but the neo-Nazis won't feel safe until the sniper is laid to rest. I can't extend any police protection to him."

The story of the clinic shooting didn't stay in the papers for long. A lone gunman who failed to shoot anyone and then was killed by an uninvolved party in self-defense didn't make big waves in New York City.

That's not to say it passed unnoticed by Herman Midler. He read Leslie's coverage over several times. Two things bothered him. For one, Cummings had not been considered unstable. The story didn't expand on that aspect of the shooting. Secondly, the person being chased by Cummings was not identified by name. He was only described as an innocent bystander.

Midler smelled a rat. The Nugent woman was controlling the facts. Cummings had obviously been there to assassinate a person he'd identified as the sniper. He was unsuccessful but his effort had identified the sniper for a future killer. Nugent knew the bystander's identity and so did a few police officers.

The shooting story indicated the name of the officer in charge of the crime scene, Officer Gentry. It also said that the "bystander" had been minimally wounded and received some care on the spot from an EMT. Midler had two avenues to pursue. He only needed one. Officer Gentry was easily contacted and had recorded the name of the bystander in his notepad. Midler represented himself as a reporter from the *Daily News* and found Gentry quite cooperative.

CHAPTER SEVENTY-FOUR

The two of them were sitting in their familiar living room. Terry had cooked dinner for them. They'd discussed the possibility of coming back together on a permanent basis. Bert knew he'd put off long enough the matter of his horrendous past. He had to tell Terry the whole truth and bear the consequences. The presence of the bracelet couldn't be ignored.

She was stunned when he told her. She began to hyperventilate. And tears began to flow.

"I'm finding it hard to absorb all this, Bert. I'm not in denial. It's just that one moment we're looking forward to a beautiful reconciliation and the next moment we're confronted by an exploding bombshell in our midst."

Bert tried to imagine what a shock it must be for Terry. His love for *her* was not changed in any way. Her love for him, though, was experiencing an enormous challenge. He hoped that their love could survive the stunning revelation.

"Terry, I'm not going to gloss over this shocking confession. What's done is done. I can't undo *any* of it. This bracelet on my ankle is at the insistence of the police. I told them the sniper was finished, but they insisted on knowing my whereabouts in case the sniper resumed activity. I understand their position.

"It's you I'm concerned about, Terry, and how you're defining *us* in this new context." He looked at her with an imploring expression.

"You've shaken me to my roots, Bert. This is maddening." She stopped and tried unsuccessfully to staunch her tears. "My first reaction tonight was not to lose what we were able to recreate between us. On further reflection, though, I see the impossibility of a normal life for us, much less one full of love and mutual respect.

I know you were hoping for a miracle, Bert. That's not in the cards for us. The damage has been done and, as you said, you can't undo any of it."

She paused and looked at Bert. He was drained of emotion. His face and sagging posture reflected it. It was as if she had let the life out of his body.

"For both our sakes this will be our last time together. You can trust me. Your secret is safe with me. Regrettably, I still love you..... but that love will have to stay dormant for all time. I'm so sorry, Bert. For you and for me."

Terry began to shake and sob. Bert's eyes filled with tears as well.

He got up, took his coat, and left the apartment without another word being said.

CHAPTER SEVENTY-FIVE

The subway ride from Bert's clinic back to the apartment he lived in alone took about twenty minutes during rush hour. The subway cars were usually crowded, and today was no exception. He exited the train at 86th Street and moved with the crowd toward the stairway up to Broadway.

A slight, non-descript middle-aged woman in a long grey coat moved closely behind him in the crowd. A sudden shock in his chest was all he felt as a bullet entered his heart from behind and ended his life. He started to fall forward in the surging crowd that briefly carried him along with it. The woman dropped her gun with its silencer and kicked it away from her. The crowd's reaction was predictable confusion. Most continued on their way to the exit and a few crowded around the fallen man. The assassin moved ahead with the exiting contingent.

Lionel Cobb got the call down by the East River where the police were pulling a van out of the depths. It was two months since he and Leslie had set in motion the plan to give Alder an opportunity to try returning to mainstream life. The sniper had been inactive.

He called her with the news.

"Leslie, here, Lionel. What's up?"

"Got news for you, Leslie. Bert Alder was shot and killed in the subway on his way home this evening. Looks like an assassination, pure and simple."

He could hear her breathing but no words were coming out.

"Are you okay, Leslie?"

"Yeah. We knew this was possible. I guess I had unreasonable hopes for Bert."

She was quiet for a moment but then continued. "This really hurts, Lionel. I've lived so long and so close to the sniper that my emotions have gotten entangled with the story."

He knew she was genuinely saddened and, to his surprise, he admitted to a similar emotion. The death of a serial killer wouldn't normally invoke this kind of response from the Chief of Homicide, but this one was different. Sharing the case with Leslie had allowed her emotional involvement to penetrate his toughened shell.

After several days' reflection, Leslie realized she was now free to write the full story and finally reveal the sniper's identity. Her editor told her the publisher would give her all the time she needed to write a book about the sniper. She wanted Gary in the project with her. His contribution had been considerable. The editor agreed.

CHAPTER SEVENTY-SIX

Leslie stood alongside Terry as Bert's coffin was lowered into the ground next to the grave of Sophie Alder. His mother had unwittingly molded her son into a vengeful killer. His wife had fallen out of love with him but came to love him anew as his character grew and his passion emerged. And then the third woman in his life, a reporter, had relentlessly pursued the sniper, heroically saved his life, and eventually came to truly care about him.

Lionel Cobb stood apart from the mourners.

ACKNOWLEDGMENTS

This book is a work of pure fiction. It was helped along by several readers who kept me from straying far off course where expert help was needed. Roberta Goodman, a good friend and therapist, was a valuable advisor where I needed to deepen my understanding of the sniper's psychopathology. Paula Most (my wife) helped me keep the female conversations realistic from the woman's point of view. Lastly, Pete King, another good friend and writer, was a voice of reason who challenged me on a number of plot inventions.

To these three people I am deeply grateful.

ABOUT THE AUTHOR

A.S. Most is a retired cardiologist with a passion for mystery/thrillers. Harlan Coben and Michael Connelly are among his favorite authors. *The Sniper* is Most's third novel. He is also the author of *No Loose Ends* and *A Deadly Cover*. Most resides in Rhode Island with his artist/educator wife. He has two sons, one an attorney and the other a journalist. He is actively working on his fourth book.

www.ingramcontent.com/pod-product-compliance
Lightning Source LLC
Chambersburg PA
CBHW051509260626
47162CB00008B/2887